NIGHT CALLS THE HUNTER—
AND THE HUNTED . . .

I don't like this, I thought. But I kept on going.

At last I came to the room where the TV still played, its voice a low mutter and its pallid light flickering. The smell I'd noticed before was all over everything now. I felt the hair rise up on the back of my neck.

I wanted to leave, but I couldn't. I had to find out—I had to talk to Elise. I stepped into the room, flashlight shining ahead of me, and then halted.

Two middle-aged people sat on the couch, staring with wide, unblinking eyes at the moving pictures on the television screen. They were dead, their necks twisted at unnatural angles, and the fronts of their clothes stained with dried blood.

For a few seconds, all I could do was stand there. I'd come here to find out how my friend Elise could be a vampire without her parents knowing.

It looked like I'd just found out . . .

Books by Debra Doyle and James D. Macdonald

BAD BLOOD
HUNTERS' MOON

HUNTERS' MOON

DEBRA DOYLE & JAMES D. MACDONALD

BERKLEY BOOKS, NEW YORK

HUNTERS' MOON

A Berkley Book / published by arrangement with
the authors

PRINTING HISTORY
Berkley edition / November 1994

ISBN: 0-425-14362-7

BERKLEY®
Berkley Books are published by The Berkley Publishing Group,
200 Madison Avenue, New York, New York 10016.
"Berkley" and the "B" logo
are trademarks belonging to the Berkley Publishing Corporation.

PRINTED IN THE UNITED STATES OF AMERICA

10 9 8 7 6 5 4 3 2 1

Chapter One

MY NAME is Val Sherwood, and I'm a lycanthrope. That's a werewolf, for all of you not-so-furry types out there.

I'm also a junior at Hillside High—and if you have to ask which one of those two things causes me the most physical pain and mental anguish . . . well, all I can say is you've never been in high school.

Think about it. Being a wolf only takes up one night every lunar month. School, on the other hand, has got me all day every day, five days a week and two hundred and seventy days a year, give or take a couple of snow days. And once the full moon goes down, I don't have to be a wolf again until the next time. No such luck with your basic school-going teenaged me: five foot three and skinny all over.

As wolves go, I'm a fairly big specimen, especially for a female. For a human, unfortunately, the same body mass translates out into something fairly small. If I were drop-dead gorgeous like my old friend Diana from junior high, nobody would ever notice; if I were somebody like my new friend Elise Barbizon—pale and delicate, like my grandmother's bone china cups—nobody would care.

I'd first met Elise Barbizon that summer, in the public library. It was right after my first year in high school, at a time when I was feeling short of friends, long on bad luck, and generally disgusted with the world. Di was still at her private school on the East Coast and planning to spend the summer in Maine with her relatives; to make things worse, I'd only gotten two letters from her since last December. Neither letter had said a word about what had happened the previous summer, when I got the bite that made me into my current sometime-furry self—and when Jay Collins, the werewolf that did it, tried to kill everybody in our old junior high crowd who knew his secret. He was two down and three to go before the rest of us stopped him.

I couldn't blame Di for wanting to forget about all that, but I sure didn't think it was fair that she and Freddie Hanger—who'd been through the bad times right along with me—got the chance to forget and I didn't. However much the stuff with Jay might have messed up their heads, at least neither one of them was out wearing a custom-made fur coat once a month, every month. Something like that makes it real hard not to believe that bad things are real.

Between one thing and another, I'd spent most of my sophomore year feeling grouchy and stand-offish, not to mention lonesome. My grades stayed up, mostly because I didn't have anything else to do with my time—and, I suppose, because I thought that doing well in school would prove that I was a good person. Burying myself in classwork and doing without a social life meant that I'd been spending a lot of time in the town library, and the habit stuck even after school let out in June.

The day I met Elise, I was in the fiction section, looking for something thick to get me through the hot-weather doldrums. Elise was sitting between two of the stacks on one of the librarians' foot-stools, with a pile of books on the floor next to her, and I'm ashamed to say that my first thought was, *That's impossible. She's too pretty. She can't really read that much.*

But there she was, her perfect, zit-free nose buried deep in a copy of *The Three Musketeers*. She glanced up from the page when I came close enough for her to hear me, and followed my gaze back down to the book again.

"Oh," she said, "did you need this one?"

I shook my head. In fact, I *had* been thinking about checking out *The Three Musketeers* and reading it again, just for the pleasure of fighting imaginary duels with the Cardinal's Guards all over seventeenth-century France, but I couldn't see snatching the book out of her fingers to do

3

it. "Don't worry," I said. "I'll read *The Count of Monte Cristo* instead."

I almost didn't say anything else—the easy thing would have been just to take a book off the shelf and go about my business—but it wasn't every day I ran into somebody who shared my taste in reading material. Instead I nodded at the book she had in her lap and said, "If you like that one, they've got *Twenty Years After* and all the other sequels. Nobody ever checks them out, either."

"It's got sequels?" she said. "That's great. I'm going to need to fill some time."

"I haven't seen you around before," I said, with my usual social charm. "I thought I knew everyone who hung out in here."

"My family moved into town last week, and I'm still wearing the new off my library card."

"They've got some good stuff," I said. "Not much for research"—especially about werewolves; I'd already seen what kind of half-sense, half-nonsense items most of the so-called "source-books" had in them—"but a lot of really great fiction."

We got to talking after that, about books we liked and so forth. She was at the library a lot that summer; I kind of got the feeling she didn't stay home much if she could help it. When I asked about the rest of her family, she didn't say much. I wondered if there was some kind of problem there, but you have to know somebody more than a few weeks before they'll talk to you

4

about things like that. I mean—I hadn't told her everything about *my* life, either.

I did find out that she was going to be a junior at Hillside High, just like I was, and when school started we turned out to have the same lunch period and a lot of the same classes. I still didn't have much of a social life, but once she'd settled in, Elise had enough social life for two people. Before long she was dating Steve Barnett, who was good-looking enough and popular enough that some of the girls were jealous.

I would have been jealous myself if I'd thought I had a prayer of attracting somebody like Steve. As it was, when it came to the dating thing I wasn't really sure *what* I thought about Elise. She was from California, for starters, and she'd grown up in a lot bigger city than anyplace I was used to. I envied her because she didn't have any trouble acting clever and sophisticated, just like the high-school kids on television. She had the right accent for it, and all the right clothes. And the looks, of course, like I said before. If she hadn't also been a lot of fun to hang around with—not to mention being the only other kid I'd ever met who'd actually read *The Prisoner of Zenda*—I might have been too intimidated by her even to say hello.

She didn't have that many other female friends at Hillside (well, neither did I, these days, so that was one place where we were even) but as far as boys were concerned it was a different matter. By October she and Steve were what my

5

grandmother would probably have called a hot number—nothing official, you understand, but spending a lot of time in each other's company. If Steve hadn't had second lunch period instead of first, I'd probably have spent all that autumn dining in lonely splendor at an otherwise empty table. Or maybe not. Elise would have been perfectly capable of dragging Steve over to join us if she felt like it.

Or me over to join him—Elise was also crazy enough not to care which way something like that went. And she definitely thought I was hiding my social light under a tightly woven bushel basket. So I should have known what she was up to the Friday in October when she said at lunch that she and Steve were going to the movies that night and having pizza afterward.

"Have a good time," I said, without much enthusiasm. I haven't felt the same about pizza since I turned werewolf—too much garlic. There's something about having your stomach trying to heave itself inside out that kills your appreciation for Italian cooking. The worst of it is, I really used to like the stuff—I've got a lot of fond memories of the way it used to taste.

Elise gave me an impatient glance. "Hey, Val— I'm asking if you'd like to come along."

I shook my head. "Sorry," I said. "I don't have a date."

Even though Elise was my friend, I sort of mumbled that last bit. Friday night is the big night around town, and if you don't have a date you're supposed to be off hiding somewhere. Showing up in public by yourself means that you don't have any friends.

Elise wasn't in a mood to take excuses, though. "So ask someone to come with you."

I put down my cheeseburger and stared at her. "*Ask* someone?"

"You heard me," said Elise. "Come on, Val. This is the nineties. Girls can ask guys out if they want to."

I wasn't sure what to say next. It looked like Elise was going to drag me into the social scene whether I wanted to be there or not—what else are friends for, after all?—and was only waiting for me to name a likely guy. I didn't want to disappoint her, but right then the only boy that I could think of was Freddie Hanger. And Freddie . . . well, he'd been a dependable friend ever since first grade—one of the few people in town who knew about my secret life as a wolf— but I don't think he'd figured out yet that I was a girl.

One other thing about Freddie: he'd put a silver bullet into me one night last autumn, mostly by accident when things got confusing. He owed me for that, and I'd never collected. Maybe now was the time.

"I think I can ask someone," I told Elise slowly. "But listen, if we do this, no pizza, okay?"

"No pizza?" Elise looked startled. I didn't blame her. Not liking pizza is practically un-American, besides being enough of a social handicap to kill you on Friday nights.

"It's a food allergy," I said. "Garlic makes me sick to my stomach."

Elise looked at my formerly full lunch tray. "I'd take your garlic allergy in a heartbeat," she said, "as long as I could get your metabolism along with it."

That's another thing about being a lycanthrope: it takes a lot of energy. We're tough; our bodies can heal themselves almost instantly; we've got more strength and speed and stamina than anybody looking at one of us would guess. But the fuel for all of that neat stuff has to come from somewhere, and I spend a big part of my time being hungry. Today I'd gone back for seconds on the cheeseburger and thirds on the fries. Sometimes I wonder how I'd handle it if getting enough food in human shape were ever a serious problem.

Elise's tray had a salad and a glass of water on it, and she'd barely touched either one. "Your own metabolism is just fine," I told her. "Believe me, you don't want mine."

"Well, I don't want mine, either. Everything I eat goes right to my hips."

I didn't try to argue with her, even though as far as her hips went, I'd seen pencils with more excess fat on them. But you couldn't convince Elise of that if you told her so until Christmas. So I said instead, "How do you go about asking a guy for a date? I've never done it."

"Since it's for tonight," Elise said, "you don't want to call after school . . . watch, I'll give you a hand. Who's going to be the lucky boy?"

Freddie had first lunch period this year. A quick glance showed me that he was sitting by himself a few tables over, eating a sandwich one-handed. With his free hand he was turning the pages of a book that he'd propped up against the salt and pepper shakers.

I gave a little nod in his direction. "How about Freddie Hanger?"

"The tall guy with the red hair? The one who's got his nose in *The Mysteries of the Supernatural*?"

"You can tell what he's reading from here?"

"No, I saw it during first period. We're in social studies together." Elise looked at him again, thoughtfully. "Well, Val, I'd say you've got decent taste. No zits, nice smile. All in all, he's not bad."

Not bad? Somehow Freddie and "not bad" didn't fit in the same sentence. I glanced over at Freddie again, trying to look beyond the freckle-faced, Dennis-the-Menace clone with braces that I'd known ever since grade school. It was, as my dad would say, an enlightening experience. Freddie had definitely changed.

Oh, the freckles were still there, all right— but the braces were gone, and sometime between last year and this one he'd gotten taller. He'd been an inch or so shorter than me when school let out in June, but he certainly wasn't shorter now. And with my luck, he'd keep right on growing, while I stayed five foot three and a quarter inches for the rest of my unnatural life.

Now Elise was watching me with an expectant expression.

"So are you going to ask him, or not?"

"I don't know."

"It's now or never—the bell is going to ring any minute."

"I don't know how to do it."

"Then watch me." She got up and went over to where Freddie was sitting, talked with him for a minute, then came back.

"He's picking you up at six," she said. "And no pizza. We'll think of something else."

Chapter
Two

AT A quarter to six that evening I was ready. I'd already changed out of my school things into what I hoped were casual-date clothes, not that I'd had all that many casual dates. Now I was wandering from the living room to the front hall and back, sitting down on the edge of the sofa for a little bit, then getting up and wandering around some more.

Stupid, I told myself. *This is Freddie, remember? Old pal, stuck with you through thick and thin, not to mention fur and fangs . . . he's not going to turn around and run if your jeans have the wrong designer label on them.*

I didn't listen to myself, though; I went and checked out my reflection in the front hall mirror anyway. Then I came back into the living room and sat down again, feeling depressed.

My dad was sitting in the armchair reading the newspaper. He looked at me over the top edge of the entertainment section and raised his eyebrows. "Something wrong?"

I sighed. "Nothing that a fashion transplant wouldn't cure."

"There's nothing wrong with the way you look, Valerie."

There wasn't anything dazzlingly *right*, either, which was the real problem—I mean, I don't break any mirrors, but nobody's ever going to mistake me for a supermodel. My grandmother says I look just like she did at my age, my dad says I have good bones, and the girls' PE coach at the high school says it's a pity I'm too short for basketball, and why don't I go out for field hockey instead?

Right. As if I didn't have enough problems.

I frowned at the toes of my good pair of sneakers. "The next thing I know, you're going to be telling me that I look 'fresh and wholesome.' Or maybe 'healthy.' You make me sound like some kind of girl jock."

"Isn't it possible, Val, that you're unfairly stereotyping the girls in the athletic programs?"

My dad's a shrink, which means he talks like that once in a while, even when he's at home. He can't help it, I guess; it's probably a reflex or something. He's okay most of the time, though, and I think he's done a pretty good job of raising me—my mother died while Dad was still in medical school, so he and Grandmother brought me up between them. Grandmother lived with us until just over a year ago, when she told us that I was big enough to do without a baby-sitter and moved to a condo in Florida.

"They're wonderful people," I said. "But I don't fit in with that crowd, either. I'd have to pretend that I really cared about scoring a few points higher, or jumping a few inches farther—and if I did try my hardest, I'd be cheating."

"The Clark Kent Syndrome," said my dad, straight-faced. He knows about the werewolf thing, which helps a lot (although telling him about it hadn't exactly been one of the high points of my life to date, and the rest of that particular evening had been even worse).

I laughed in spite of being nervous. "Just buy me some long underwear and sew a bright red *S* on the front," I said, and right about then I heard the sound of a pickup truck pulling into the driveway.

Freddie knocked on the front door and I let him in. He looked two or three times as well-scrubbed and polished as I'd ever seen him, and he said, "Good evening, sir," to my father as if they'd never met before, all formal and polite. My father was formal and polite right back—it was probably some kind of guy thing, because it seemed to satisfy both of them—and then Dad made all the usual parent noises at me: "What time are you going to be home?" and "Have a good time," and so on.

Then Freddie and I got into the clunker he was driving these days—a rusted-out Ford pickup that had been doing farm work for almost as long as Freddie had been alive. The cab of the pickup was dusty and smelled faintly of motor oil and sweat. The floor was littered with the crumpled pages of old school papers; the vinyl seat cover had cracked and split open a long time ago, and somebody had mended the split with silvery duct tape.

"Sorry about the mess," Freddie said.

"Don't worry about it," I said. "At least it's all yours. I have to drive Dad's Toyota if I want to go anywhere."

The pickup seemed to suit Freddie's character—not fancy, but practical, with surprising things tucked in out-of-the-way corners. I found myself staring out the window and thinking that he wasn't just a friend: I actually liked him. It surprised me.

"Nice night," I said finally. It sounded lame and I knew it. Just listening to myself was enough to make me start despairing all over again. *Real original, Teen Wonder.*

Freddie nodded. "Not too cold yet."

He sounded as tongue-tied as I felt. You'd have thought the two of us had met for the first time yesterday, instead of knowing each other since practically forever. But we'd never gone out on a date before, which made all the difference. I'd probably never be able to talk to him like a normal human being again, and it was all Elise's fault.

I'll get you for this, Elise Barbizon, I really will.

I didn't say anything for a minute or two. After a while, Freddie spoke up—I guess he thought it was his turn to make conversation.

"Did you have a good summer?" he asked. He was concentrating real hard on the road ahead, even though there wasn't any traffic. I wondered if he was hoping to find cue cards hidden in the stoplights—"How to Talk With Your Date," lessons one through twelve, with sample dialogues, just like in French class at school.

He ought to save his energy. I've already looked, and there's nothing up there.

"It was okay," I said. "Not much happened. I took drivers' ed in summer school and got my license, but that's about all. How about you?"

"I made it to September in one piece," he said. "That's good enough for me these days." He hesitated. "You said not much happened. Does that mean you're still—"

"Turning into a wolf once a month at the full moon?" I really wished he hadn't brought that up, just when I was starting to feel like a normal teenager for a change. Scared paralytic at the thought of going out on a date with a guy I'd known since before I could tie my own shoelaces, but normal. "Yeah, I'm still doing that. Sorry."

"It's okay, honest." He was quiet again for a while, and then he said, "I just wondered—you wouldn't happen to know where the local predators hang out, would you? Coyotes, wild dogs, that sort of thing?"

"No," I said bluntly. "I don't run with them, and they stay away from me."

"Sorry," he said again, and went back to staring at the road.

After a few seconds I started to get curious. Freddie had actually sounded like he needed an answer to that question—it hadn't come out of the usual small-talk storage bin, that was for sure.

"Why do you want to know?" I asked. "Is there something going on that I haven't heard about?"

He shrugged. "Problems with the livestock. I thought maybe you'd noticed something, is all."

"No," I said. "I don't go out in that direction anyway. Sorry."

After that he dropped the subject, and we spent the rest of the way to the movie theater talking about the high school football team's chances for making it to the regional championship. I didn't care one way or another about it, and I don't think Freddie did, either, but it was safe.

We kept on like that, talking about nothing in particular, as if we'd only met a few weeks before instead of knowing each other for years, until we got to the six-screen theater at the mall. Elise and Steve were already in the ticket line when we got there. We joined them, and spent the time laughing and talking about school and TV and all kinds of silly stuff until we got up to the box office.

There wasn't anything big playing this week, so we'd pretty much decided to see whatever movie was starting closest to the time when we got our tickets, which turned out to be a PG-rated comedy starring no one I'd ever heard of. That was still better than waiting fifteen minutes to see machine guns and exploding cars, and I didn't argue. Freddie insisted on buying the tickets, which didn't seem quite fair considering that the whole thing had been my idea in the first place, or maybe Elise's—so I insisted on buying the popcorn and sodas and hot dogs and chocolate-covered raisins, which all together cost more than the tickets had, so I figured we were sort of even.

It took us a while to find seats and get ourselves and our junk food all sorted out. Elise hadn't gotten anything, which didn't surprise me much—I'd have been more surprised if she had—but the rest of us had to juggle quite a load of stuff. Eventually we found ourselves a place in the middle of the theater and settled down to watch the feature.

I wanted to watch the flick. I tried. But I couldn't concentrate on the movie. I couldn't concentrate on my date, either. I'd had hopes of getting my hand held, at least, but even though I kept the hand nearest Freddie palm up and empty he wouldn't get the hint. But more than that, I felt a pair of eyes watching me from somewhere in the dark behind us. I could feel them on the back of my neck, staring. It was spooky. I tried to tell myself that it was just imagination, but that didn't work.

17

After a while it got so bad that I couldn't sit still any longer. I mumbled something about going to the ladies' room, just so I could get up and walk out to the lobby and come back, checking out the rest of the crowd. I've got good night vision, even in human shape—it's one of lycanthropy's little plusses, to go along with all the stuff on the minus side—but I didn't see anybody who made the hairs rise up on the back of my neck.

I gave up and sat back down. Someone was still watching. I could feel it, like eyes behind me in the dark. But now the eyes were watching somebody else.

What with one thing and another, I was glad to see the final credits roll. I'd had about all of that movie theater I could take. I didn't mention how I felt to any of the others; I knew already that it wasn't something they would understand. But even a once-a-month predator like me can tell when something bigger and nastier is hunting in the neighborhood. Our town may not be very big by California standards, but it's not too small to have a crime problem, and I was glad I wouldn't be walking home alone tonight.

After the movie, the four of us went to an ice cream parlor for sandwiches and hot fudge sundaes. It's a good thing that werewolves aren't allergic to chocolate. I can live without garlic and silver, but if I had to give up chocolate . . . I don't want to think about it.

Freddie and I said good-bye to Steve and Elise in the ice cream place. My weekend curfew was a lot earlier than Elise's, which was a problem Dad and I were going to have to work out in detail one of these days. My father's pretty reasonable about things like that; on the other hand, he has this inconvenient habit of expecting me to be reasonable about them, too.

"See you Monday," I said to Elise before I left the table. "And be careful going home, okay?"

Elise just laughed. "I grew up in the city," she said. "I'm always careful. Besides, I've got Steve to watch over me."

"Whatever works for you," I said. "Have fun."

Freddie drove me home. When we got there the porch light was on. We stood on the front step—close enough together that I had to turn my face up if I wanted to look at him—and for a moment I thought maybe the evening was going to amount to something after all.

Nothing happened, though, except that Freddie's ears slowly turned bright red. Finally he muttered something that sounded like "thank-you-for-a-nice-evening," and all but ran back to his pickup. I watched him drive away, then turned around and went into the house.

Dad was in the living room reading a magazine—not real subtle, but then I hadn't gone out on dates all that often. I tossed my purse onto the couch, then sat down next to it and stretched out my legs. Dad glanced up from his magazine.

"Have a good time, Val?"

"I guess."

I must not have sounded very happy, because he said, "Anything go wrong that I ought to know about?"

There was a hunter stalking someone in the movie theater, and Freddie Hanger didn't kiss me good night.

"No," I said aloud.

He looked dubious. "Are you sure? Remember, I was in high school once myself. Granted, it was a long time ago . . ."

"That's what you keep telling me," I said. "Were the rocks cool yet?"

"Mostly," he said. "But it was rough living on nothing but single-cell plants. Anyway, back when I was your age, I hated the whole dating scene. The things people put themselves through in the name of having a good time. . . . I'm amazed that I didn't become a hermit."

My dad talking about himself? Something odd was going on. But he was already back on track and talking about my problems again.

"You seemed a bit unhappy about something when you first came in," he said. "Anything you'd like to talk about?"

I shook my head. "Nothing serious."

"You're sure?"

"I'm sure," I said. I didn't feel like explaining that the phrase, "sweet sixteen and never been kissed," had lost its charm for me several months back.

Hillside High is full of kids my age doing absolutely everything they can think of on a daily

*basis, but yours truly the Teen Werewolf can't
even find someone to hold hands with.*

I didn't say that, either. My dad likes to think
that he's guaranteed postmodern unshockable,
but he saves that for his office hours. Where
his baby girl is concerned, he's nowhere near as
sympathetic.

I meant what I said, though, when I told him
the problem wasn't serious. I'd seen what serious life-and-death problems looked like, back
last year when I was brand-new to the lycanthrope game. I'd lost a couple of good friends
permanently that way, and another friend—the
gorgeous Di—was still trying to forget that the
whole thing had ever happened.

I didn't have that option, unfortunately. Every
time the full moon came around, I turned into
a living, breathing, fur-covered reminder that
werewolves exist. Jay Collins had been a werewolf, and a killer, until Diana had put a silver
bullet into his head. I wasn't like Jay, or at least
I sure hoped I wasn't. But wondering about it
tended to have a sobering effect on me sometimes, and it certainly helped give me a sense
of proportion. Compared to some of the things
that could happen to people, a dud evening at
the movie theater wasn't all that bad.

Chapter
Three

I WENT to my room and stayed up way too late listening to tapes on my headphones. I went to sleep eventually, and had dreams all night about flying high above the town and looking down on the people who lived there, like I could see right through the roofs and see where they were sleeping.

In my dreams, the moon was nearly full. It filled my room with light. I could feel the moon calling to me, trying to make me change, trying to make me one of the things that run through the night. I could taste fresh blood in my mouth, something more than rabbit's blood. I wanted to kill and drink blood.

I stirred restlessly, coming half-awake for a little while, before I drifted back again into sleep. For a while, in my dream, I was in my own house, moving through empty rooms washed with a pale half-light from the high, blank-faced moon.

In the dream, I heard a knock sounding at

the front door. Soft, like a tree branch tapping against a windowpane, but I knew—the way you know things in dreams—that it wasn't the wind, but someone who wanted to talk to me.

The rest of the house was full of a deep, motionless silence. From the faraway vantage point of sleep, I watched as my dream-self padded barefoot along the hall, past the living room, to the front door, and pulled it open.

The man who stood on the threshold could have been a lawyer, or a banker, or anything else respectable. Even in the faint illumination of the corner streetlight, his tailored grey suit looked like something out of an ad for high-performance sports cars, and his clean-shaven face was nothing unusual, either.

"Good evening, Valerie," the stranger said. "How pleasant to find you at home."

There was nothing remarkable about his voice, except that I couldn't have stopped listening to it if I'd wanted to. But his eyes . . . they were blank, like marble. They caught and held me, and I couldn't look away.

"Won't you invite me in?" he asked.

I stood there, dressed in my pajamas, with the cold October wind blowing. The man in the grey suit looked back at me.

I opened my mouth to say "Go away!" and slam the door. My mind thought the words, and I opened my mouth to say them.

"Would you like to come in?" I said.

He smiled.

"Thank you, no," he said. "Not now. Perhaps another time."

And he was gone. I stood on the doorstep for a long time, in my dream, feeling afraid and—at the same time—abandoned.

Then the substance of my dreams changed again, into the dim grey-and-white images and the vivid impressions of scent and touch that meant my dream-self was running in wolf-shape. The wolf-dreams were familiar ones, and comforting in their simplicity. I let them lead me back into deeper, and finally dreamless, sleep.

I slept late the next morning, and woke up feeling grouchy and fuzzy-headed. My mood didn't improve much over the weekend, especially when I didn't hear from either Freddie or Elise. I didn't feel like talking to Freddie, but by Sunday afternoon I was so bored I called up Elise just to chat.

That didn't do any good, either. All I got was her mother, who said, "I'm sorry, but Elise can't come to the phone right now," in a way that made it plain Elise wasn't going to be coming to the phone any other time that day, either. I wondered what was up, but I didn't have the nerve to ask.

The rest of Sunday was a drag, and Monday, when I woke up to it, wasn't much better. Mondays never are. I ate a good breakfast anyway— Dad took one look at my face and said something about "the condemned woman ate a hearty meal."

"Jokes," I said. "On a Monday morning." I poured milk onto my second bowl of cornflakes. "Don't forget; tonight's your turn to cook dinner."

Dad looked resigned. "I remember. I've got the chicken thawing in the refrigerator right now."

My father and I have shared the kitchen chores ever since Grandmother left. In fact, she claims that one of the reasons she waited so long before moving out was that she had to make certain Dad learned how to cook first. Neither one of us is up to her standard—I do a pretty good meat loaf and a couple of boring casseroles, and my dad does fast things with poultry pieces and store-bought sauce—but we manage to get by with only a little help from the microwave and the take-out places down by the mall.

"I can hardly wait," I said. "Better get it started early, though. Tonight's . . ."

I didn't finish the sentence. Like I said, Dad knows about me—he even believes in what he knows, which took some serious mental rearrangement on his part. But it still isn't something we talk about very much.

"Right," he said. "If I'm late getting out of the office, I'll pick up something from the deli on the way home. We can always hold off on the chicken until tomorrow."

"Anything but Italian," I said. I finished the last of my cereal and drank a final glass of milk, then collected my purse and schoolbooks from the kitchen counter and headed for the door.

"Time for me to run if I want to catch the bus."

The bus stop is just down the street from our house. Hillside is a big consolidated high school; a lot of the kids from our neighborhood take the city buses to get there. That saves the rattly old yellow school buses for the students who live way out of town on the rural routes—people like Freddie, until he'd gotten wheels.

The air outside was fresh and crisp, with a deep blue sky and enough wind to ruffle my hair around my face. A perfect autumn day—and according to the weather report, tonight was going to be a perfect autumn night. I felt a pleasant prickle of anticipation as I sniffed the breeze. Oh, yes, tonight would be fine. If you've never run on four legs across the hilltops under a bright moon, you can't imagine how fine. Sometimes I wonder what it would be like to run the hills by daylight, but I can't do that, any more than I can stop the change when the time comes. I knew another lycanthrope once—a wise old wolf—who could hold off the change when he had to; but I wasn't that good, and even he couldn't keep himself in wolf-shape once the moon was down.

The bus got me to Hillside about ten minutes before the first bell. Everybody was still waiting around outside. I spotted Freddie and gave him a "Hi there," and a wave; he waved back but didn't leave the group he was standing with, mostly other boys from Future Farmers of America and the Metals shop. Freddie's

a bit highbrow for that crowd, if you ask me—
but Freddie hadn't, so I went on past and found
Elise to talk to instead.

"Hi," I said. "How's it going?"

"Not so hot. I'm grounded." She didn't sound
worried about it.

I was startled for a moment, until I remembered how her mother had sounded on Sunday
afternoon. But I was still curious. "Grounded?
What for?"

"Remember last Friday?" Elise grinned at me.
"I didn't get back until past my curfew."

Something about her expression made me curious. Elise didn't look like someone who was in
trouble with her family; she looked smug. "How
far past your curfew?"

She giggled. "Like about dawn Saturday."

"You're kidding," I said. "My dad would kill me
if I tried something like that."

Elise just shrugged. "I don't care what my parents think."

I decided it was time to change the subject. I
nodded toward the book Elise had been reading
when I came up: *Have His Carcase*, by Dorothy
Sayers.

"Is that from the library or is it one of yours?"

"Mine," she said. "Us grounded people don't
have a chance to go to the library."

"It was a dumb thing to do," I said. So I hadn't
managed to change the subject yet. That sort of
thing is harder than it looks, especially when
you're still curious about what went on. "You

must have known your parents would notice when you didn't come in."

She just smiled. "It was worth it."

I shook my head. *With Steve Barnett?* I thought. Aloud, I just said, "If you say so."

Not that I was likely to find out any different, the way my social life had been going lately. And not that I could get away with anything like staying out all night—well, I *was* getting away with something like that, but in wolf-skin it's different. No Steve Barnett, for one thing.

About then the bell rang, and the students started pouring in through the doors of Hillside High like beans through a funnel. The day was just an average school day—pre-calc, English, French, world history, chemistry, and gym—and I managed to stay alert clear through to the end in spite of all the distractions. I'm always edgy on the day of a change; it's harder to concentrate, and everything seems to smell and taste and feel sharper somehow, as if I had a layer of skin missing. But I've been a lycanthrope for a year now, and I'm learning how to cope.

Writing notes to myself, for example: UNFASTEN SCREEN WINDOW (because paws can't do that trick) and PUT DOWN OLD BEDSPREAD. The thermometer was supposed to drop tonight, and I'd be chilly after I made the change back to human shape. Also muddy all over, if past experience was any guide. Best to stay off the good linen; if I got it dirty, I'd be the one who had to wash it.

The last class was finally over, and I took the

bus home. As soon as I got there, I went into the kitchen for an after-school snack. I never can persuade the lunchroom ladies to give me large enough portions; they all take one look at me and decide that I probably don't eat enough to keep a bird alive. Roast beef sandwich in hand, I settled down at the kitchen table to do my pre-calc homework. I'm usually not so virtuous that I do all my assignments first thing, but I knew that if I waited until evening my mind wouldn't want to focus on anything as abstract as math.

Even in mid-afternoon, I could feel the tug of the coming moonrise. I'd found out by now that fighting it didn't help. I just had to pace myself—doing a problem, then getting up and moving restlessly around the house for a few minutes before settling down again and tackling the next one.

It was during one of my spells of prowling that I spotted the moving van. My first thought was that it was awfully late in the day for movers— almost five-thirty already, and it looked like take-out food for dinner tonight, because Dad still hadn't shown up—and my second thought was, *Who on earth travels with their shrubbery?* I mean, it isn't often that you see a loaded moving van with a full-grown lilac bush wrapped in burlap and strapped to the back.

The moving van rolled on past, turning left at the corner and heading out of sight. Wherever the owner of the lilac bush was planning to live, it wasn't on our street. I watched the van go, then shrugged—there's no telling what some people think is important enough to haul across the country with them—and went back to my math.

I only had one more problem left to go, and I was finishing it up when my dad came in. He was carrying a couple of white paper bags with a red-and-black logo on them: THE CLEVER GOURMET.

"New place?" I asked.

"Just opened." He set the bags down on the counter and started taking out white cardboard tubs and boxes. "It's got the downstairs front in that renovated Victorian place across from my office."

"Real convenient." I sniffed the air. "How are they on things like garlic?"

"Not in any of these," he said. He put one of the flat, square tubs into the microwave. "I checked. Regina says she likes the challenge of working with the more understated seasonings."

"Regina?"

I could have sworn he looked sheepish. "Ms. Polidori. She and her brother run the shop together."

"You must have had quite a chat."

"We talked a bit while she was packaging things up," Dad admitted. "The Polidoris just moved here from New York. Regina says that the whole East Coast is so thick with upscale catering services that a new business doesn't stand a chance."

I thought of saying something sarcastic about missionaries bringing civilization into the wilderness, but the food in the microwave smelled too good for me to do it. Dad had picked out chicken breasts in some kind of creamy, dill-flavored sauce, and I had to admit that Regina Polidori—or her brother, if he was the chef—could certainly cook.

I finished my share of the chicken and sopped up what was left of the sauce with a bit of crusty sourdough bread on the end of a fork. It all tasted so delicious that I dawdled over the end of the meal a bit longer than I should have. I had to put down my fork and stand up in a hurry when I saw how much darker it had gotten.

"Um . . . sorry to leave you with the dishes when it's my turn," I said, edging for the door. "I'll do dinner and dishes both tomorrow, I promise."

I headed out the door and down the hall toward my room. The notes I'd written to myself earlier were tacked up on my bulletin board. Moving fast—I could feel the moonrise coming already—I took the screen out of the window and leaned it against the wall, then pulled the old bedspread down onto the floor on top of the hooked rug. Then I turned off the lights and undressed. Clothes don't make the change, and by the time you've tooth-and-clawed your way out of pajamas, they aren't good for much of anything anymore.

The wind coming in through the open window raised goose bumps on my bare skin, but that wouldn't last much longer. I lay down on the bedspread to wait.

I'd cut things pretty close. A minute or so later, it happened. Even after a whole year, the change was still scary and exciting at the same time—like having all the bones and nerves and muscles in my body turn to water and start flowing uphill. The room shifted around me. Wolf eyes don't see like human eyes; the perspective is different, and the colors are missing. But once the first whiff of the night comes in on the breeze, you don't even care.

I gathered my four legs under me and was out through the open window in a single jump.

The moon was just up, its top edge barely peeping above the horizon. Patchy wisps of cloud scudded across the light-washed sky. I tilted back my head and howled—partly to let Dad know that I was on my way, but mostly for the pure good feeling of it. The O'Donnells' Irish setter, Fleabrain, started barking and hurling himself against the door of the sun porch next door, just like he did every month. I howled again back at him, my wolf-thoughts laughing, and loped off into the night.

Chapter Four

THIS WAS the good part, the part that made all the rest worthwhile—the sickness from eating garlic; the rashes (like burns, almost, and getting worse as I grew older) from touching silver; and the nuisance of having to plan my day-to-day life around the phases of the moon. I could run for miles in the darkness, covering the ground in long strides, and howl to my heart's content at the harvest moon.

This is my night, and my hunting ground . . . mine!

The packs of half-wild stray dogs that ranged these hills during the rest of the month stayed away on the nights of the full moon. I owned this territory then. I caught field mice and ate them, and the other small nocturnal creatures that were any wolf's rightful meal—satisfying, for a little while, the nagging lycanthrope's hunger that never quite went away.

Tonight the rich medley of scents that filled the yard and the street had a new note in it—

vegetable, not animal; dense and unfamiliar; and mingled with it, the smell of new-turned earth. The wolf-mind tried to place it, but failed. Human memory turned up only a picture of a moving van with a lilac bush wrapped in burlap strapped to the rear bumper.

I followed the strange scent for a while; this was my neighborhood and whatever changed in it interested me. It led me away from the newer suburbs and in toward the part of town where big old Victorian Gothic houses sat on lawns the size of city blocks. Most of the houses had been remodeled into offices for lawyers and doctors—my dad's among them—but a few still had people living inside. On most nights the area smelled like a living neighborhood—a bit heavy on the rubbing alcohol and book dust, but colored with the odors of cooking and garbage, and the mixed scents of humans and pets.

Tonight, though, the air smelled subtly different, as though something about the neighborhood had changed. I prowled about, whimpering uneasily in my throat, trying to trace the source of the new and unknown scent. I didn't like it when things changed their smell without warning me.

Then the wind shifted until it was blowing from the north, and the vague wrongness became a strong smell that raised the fur along my spine and made me growl and bare my teeth: a stink like something rotten had pushed up from the ground somewhere close by, making the human part of me think of pale, unpleasant things like worms and spotted mushrooms. The wind veered east again, and the smell vanished as suddenly as it had come.

Part of me wanted to follow the trail back northward, to find what sort of thing smelled like that, but the more human part of my mind held me back. Heading northward would lead me closer to the center of town, which was no place for a right-thinking wolf to be. Too many people downtown; too many ways for my secret to come out.

I turned the other way, heading back toward the fields and foothills.

A sound of wings rustled overhead as a night-bird passed, another hunter seeking its meal for the evening. Behind me in the city, I heard a siren wailing—yet another hunter, after a different prey—but the countryside was quiet except for the low-key sounds of small animals moving through the night.

I didn't start back home until the moon began to sink toward the horizon. Then I began threading my way through the streets and highways, dodging the night-shift workers going home and the early commuters trying to get a jump on the rest of the traffic. The smell of exhaust was thick along the highways, making my eyes and throat burn. I took the last couple of blocks at a dead run as the moon seemed to fall down toward the horizon, rather than set. I leapt over the windowsill and skidded to a landing on the old bedspread.

The alarm clock woke me up an hour later. One hour wasn't really enough sleep for the school day ahead. I probably could have gotten out of classes by phoning the school office and claiming I had cramps—being a wolf isn't the only thing that comes around once a lunar month—but I didn't like the idea of lying. Besides, I still had all that lycanthropic energy and endurance to draw on if I needed it.

I hurried across the hall to take a shower and clean my teeth and fingernails. Hunting—even small stuff like rats and rabbits—can leave you pretty messy. When you're a carnivore, though, it's part of the job description; if you ask me, catching some field mice once a month isn't any worse than going after wild duck with a shotgun.

I dressed as quickly as I could, then went into the kitchen in search of breakfast. My dad was there already—mornings after the full moon he usually drives me in to school so that I can save time and sleep a few minutes later. Things like that make me glad he knows the truth about me; life in general would be a lot harder if he didn't.

The clock-radio on top of the refrigerator was tuned to the news and weather station. As I came in, the announcer was telling everybody that it would be cooler today and tonight, with a possibility of showers along toward evening, and a chance of frost tomorrow morning. I poured myself a glass of milk, drank it straight off still standing in front of the open refrigerator, then poured myself another full glass and went about getting together a bowl of cornflakes.

The announcer shifted to the news: trouble in the Middle East, trouble in Europe, trouble in Africa, trouble at home in New York and L.A. "And in the local news, three-year-old Lamont Johnson vanished last night from his family's home on Parker Road. Police report no signs of an intruder . . ."

Bad news like that, the kind with kids hurt or in trouble, always makes my dad gloomy for the rest of the day. Grandmother used to tell him he couldn't pick up every fallen sparrow in the world. He said he knew that—but as far as I could ever tell, knowing it never stopped him from wanting to try.

"Maybe I could help with that sort of thing someday," I said. Mostly, I just wanted to cheer him up. "You know, tracking lost kids."

Dad gave me a kind of preoccupied glance. "Next time someone goes missing during the full moon, I'll be sure to bring you in." He frowned at his coffee mug. "But do you really think that you could track things as well as a—"

He broke off there, looking a bit embarrassed. I wondered whether he'd been about to say "trained professional" or "real dog." Either one would have sounded silly. My bet was on "trained professional"; it's good shrinkspeak, and whenever Dad doesn't know what else to say he falls back on stuff like that.

"I don't know," I said. "I can follow a track better by smell than most cops probably can by eye, and I'm at least a little bit smarter than your average bloodhound." I took a spoonful of my cornflakes. "Of course, it might work better the other way around."

That made him laugh, which I'd hoped it would, even though I could tell he was still worried. We finished our breakfast and he drove me off to school. Nobody at Hillside knew anything about the missing kid, Elise lived near Parker Road, but she'd only been in town for a few months herself, and didn't know him or his family.

"You didn't notice anything strange going on last night?" I asked her during lunch. It was macaroni and cheese day at the cafeteria, which wasn't as meaty a meal as I would have liked, but at least the lunchroom ladies were giving out big helpings. "No tramps or prowlers or anything?"

"No," Elise said. "It was quieter than a graveyard all night long."

"It was pretty quiet down at my end of town, too." I shrugged. "We'll probably never find out what happened."

I went back to my second helping of macaroni and cheese. My stomach didn't care what might have gone on last night on Parker Road; it was still hungry. Elise, though, was eating her usual bowl of greenery from the salad bar, and not much of that. We finished lunch, then I double-checked my French homework while Elise read some more Dorothy Sayers before the bell rang for the next class period.

When I got home from school that afternoon, the search for the missing three-year-old had grown to take in the surrounding countryside. The volunteer searchers kept on looking all night and into the next afternoon, without any results, then gave up. The police marked the case down as a possible kidnapping and passed it over to the FBI.

I admit I didn't think about it too much myself; missing three-year-olds who aren't related to you aren't really one of your average high schooler's day-to-day concerns. Maybe if I'd taken serious action right then, things would have been different, because it did concern me. A lot.

But I didn't know that yet—and by the time Lamont Johnson started showing up on milk cartons, it would be way, way too late.

The rest of October went past without anything much happening. I kept on doing okay—well, actually, better than okay—in all my classes. The school football team won three more games, and people started talking like we had a chance at the district championship. Elise finished reading *Have His Carcase* and loaned it to me. And Dad brought home a lot of late dinners from the Clever Gourmet, which was fine with me. Regina Polidori—or maybe her brother—did

41

things with chicken and paprika that my grand-mother never even dreamed of.

The weather stayed fine all through the month, with crisp nights and sunny days. Trees all over town turned yellow and orange and bright red, and shed their leaves in big, crunchy drifts of color along the sidewalks.

"This is the best time of the year," I said to Elise. "Cool enough to sleep at night and warm enough in the daytime to be comfortable."

"It's too cold for me already," said Elise.

We were eating lunch in the school cafeteria, or rather I was eating lunch and Elise was picking at a cheese and fruit vegetarian plate. I thought it was too hot in the cafeteria myself— the school district turns on the central heating on the first of October every year like clockwork, no matter whether we're in the middle of a heat wave or it's been snowing since September. But Elise really did look chilly. She was wearing a thick cable-knit pullover with long sleeves and a high turtle-neck, and she shivered when she said it was too cold.

I remembered that her family had moved into town from someplace in California where the local idea of winter was a few rainy days when the thermometer dropped to sixty. "You think it's cold now," I said, "just wait until it starts snowing. *Then* you'll see some cold."

"Snow," she said, and gave a shiver. "I don't think I'm ready for snow."

"You'd better get ready real soon," I said. "Once it sticks, it's on the ground until March."

"I think I'll pull down my window shades and hibernate."

"You look like you could use the sleep," I said. And she did, too. She was so thin her wrists looked knobby coming out of the thick knitted cuffs of her sweater. Her eyes had dark circles under them, like smudges of purple against her pale skin. "Are you sure you're okay?"

"I'm fine. Honest."

I still felt worried. "You're not eating. You don't have something wrong with you, do you?"

"I'm just not very hungry today."

"You're never hungry lately," I pointed out. "Look, maybe you need to . . . well, *talk* to somebody."

"You mean a shrink? Like your dad?"

She was acting insulted. I pretended not to notice.

"Not my dad," I said. "You're a friend of a relative of his, so he'd probably refer you to somebody else."

"Val, will you just drop it? Please?"

She was starting to get really upset now. Her voice had risen, and there were red spots in her cheeks where the blood had rushed up to the surface. I didn't want to have a fight in the middle of the cafeteria—that's a one-way ticket to the principal's office and all sorts of major trouble—so I shut up and went back to eating my lunch.

43

That was my second big mistake, of course. I could see that something was wrong with Elise; ever since pulling that stunt with Steve Barnett and getting grounded she'd been acting like something right off those "Is Your Child One of Today's Troubled Teens?" checklists you see in magazines. I should have stuck with it, and dragged her in to talk with my father any way that I could. If I had . . .

I didn't have much time to think about it right then, however. Another tray clattered down onto the table, and I looked up to see my old pal Freddie Hanger. For some reason, he'd picked today to desert his usual noisy crowd of lunchtime buddies and come around to renew our acquaintance.

"Hello, Val," he said. "Long time no see. Almost a month."

"Not my fault," I said. "We go to the same school and all. And share the same lunch hour, even."

"Hey," he said. "You can walk across a room and talk to a guy without shocking people. I didn't spot any messages from you on the family answering machine, either."

I had to admit he had a point there. Girls spend enough time complaining about guys not calling them back. It was embarrassing to realize that I'd been doing—or not doing—the same thing to Freddie.

"Sorry," I said. "If I'd known you wanted to hear from me, I'd have sent a singing telegram.

How've you been doing lately?"

"Just fine." He paused. "How about you? Getting out at night very much?"

It sounded like a friendly question, but I knew what he really meant: *How's the werewolf business these days, Valerie?* I mean, he couldn't be wondering whether I was dating anybody, because I wasn't.

"I do okay for myself," I said aloud.

"How about you, Elise?" Freddie said.

She smiled at him. "Oh, I'm still new in town; I haven't gotten tired of looking at things yet."

For an instant I felt like snarling at her—*getting grounded over Steve Barnett wasn't enough; she's got to go after Freddie, too?*—because Freddie was smiling back and saying, "Well, if you need someone to show you around, you can call on me anytime."

Then Elise glanced over at me, and her expression changed. It was strange to watch, as if she'd just caught herself doing something she'd promised herself she wouldn't ever do. "I don't know—"

"That's okay. Just keep me in mind; I'm around most afternoons and weekends. Val knows my number if you want to call." He glanced at his watch. "Oops—sorry. Gotta go. It's almost time for the bell."

And he was off, leaving me and Elise to trade puzzled glances.

"Was he asking me out," Elise said finally, "or was he asking you?"

"You tell me and we'll both know," I said. I was still feeling irritated; Freddie might have shed the braces and gotten taller, but he wasn't Mr. Suave yet by a long shot. Come to think of it, I wasn't doing too well on the social-interaction stuff these days, either. "And after we've figured it out we can tell him, because I don't think he's got it straight yet himself."

Chapter
Five

WHEN I got home that day after school, I noticed that there wasn't anything thawing out for dinner. Tonight was Dad's turn to cook, which meant I could look forward to more take-out stuff. To my surprise, however, he didn't come in carrying some of those by now familiar white-red-and-black bags.

"What's for dinner?" I asked.

"Put on your glad rags," he said. "I thought we might eat out tonight, instead of carrying stuff in."

"I get the feeling," I said, "that what you've got in mind isn't exactly one of the burger joints down by the mall."

"Not a burger joint, no. There's a place outside of town—the Carson House—that I've heard good things about lately."

Curiouser and curiouser, I thought, as I went off to my room to change clothes. It's not like Dad only takes me out to places where you

47

pick your food up at the counter and carry it back to the table on a tray. I've got a couple of good dresses, and my company manners are as respectable as my grandmother could make them. But Dad tends to save the fancy dinners for special occasions, and this wasn't a holiday or my birthday or anything like that. It wasn't even a weekend. I mean, who goes out to eat on a Thursday night?

But I wasn't going to look a gift restaurant in the mouth. I put on the velvet dress that Grandmother had given me for Christmas, and that I'd worn maybe once since I got it—the Hillside High life-style isn't real big on formal weddings and nights at the opera. We got into the car and drove out to the restaurant. The Carson House was a long way out of town, all right, and when we came to the turnoff, the only sign was a square white board in a cast-iron bracket, with ENTRANCE written on it in black copperplate script.

Inside . . . well, if you'd wanted a definition of "understated elegance" for a photo dictionary, the Carson House would have worked just fine. Dad ordered some kind of roast duck in sauce, which didn't look half bad, and I had steak tartare—that's raw beef, for those of you who've never had it. They chop it up fine and serve it with black bread, and give you things like green onions to mix in. It's good, and Dad didn't ask "Are you making a statement about your identity?" and I didn't snarl at him, either.

We were waiting for the dessert cart to come around when Dad said, "Val, there's something I need to talk with you about."

"Oh?" I tried to look nothing more than politely interested. At the same time, I was hastily running through all the things that I might have had on my conscience. But for the life of me, I couldn't think of anything I'd either done or not done that was so serious it needed a dinner out to take care of. "What about? Me?"

"Well," Dad said. "Not you, exactly."

"What do you mean?"

Dad fiddled with one of the forks. "It's . . . you've probably figured out that I've been seeing someone lately."

I hadn't figured it out, in fact, and his announcement took me by surprise. I tried not to show it. "Dating, you mean?"

"Not yet," he said. "Not really. Just lunches and stuff."

About then the light finally dawned. "So this was a dress rehearsal for the real thing." Which meant I knew who it was, too. "It must be that Regina Polidori person you've been talking about, the one from the Clever Gourmet."

"Yes," he said. "I think . . . I'm rather hoping that this will turn out to be something special."

I wasn't sure how I felt about that. It wasn't that I remembered my mother—I didn't, really, just the things that Dad and Grandmother had told me about her. And I didn't really mind the idea of him dating someone, either. I could have used a date or two myself. The "something special" bit . . . that was different, because I knew what it meant. Somebody I didn't know was going to be moving into my life, whether I wanted her there or not.

I said the first thing that came into my head. "Are you going to tell her about me?"

"I can't very well pretend I don't have a teen-aged daughter," Dad said, just as the dessert cart came rolling up. "It wouldn't be fair to let the relationship develop without letting her know."

That wasn't what I'd meant, and I think he knew it. I couldn't say anything, though, as long as the waiter was standing there pointing out the chocolate mousse cake, the *baba au rhum*, and a half dozen other things I can't remember. I picked something at random, and as soon as the waiter was gone I said, "Right. Not fair. What I want to know is, *how much* are you going to tell her about me?"

I could tell from his expression that he hadn't even thought of that particular problem—which gave me a worse feeling than anything he'd said so far, because Dad's always been a big one for thinking everything through in detail before getting started. If Regina Polidori was special enough to make him leap from conversations over the take-out counter to the possibility of wedding bells without stopping to remember his lycan-thropic daughter—then he really *was* serious.

And I was mad. He'd forgotten about me. "Well?"

He'd ordered chocolate mousse cake. Now he was poking it with his fork. "You can't bring secrets into a long-term relationship, Valerie. It doesn't work."

"I don't care. It's my secret. And it *isn't* my relationship."

He sighed. "I do have a right to a life of my own, Val."

"So do I. And—what I am—is part of mine, not yours."

"Be reasonable, Valerie. If you had any other . . . problem, I'd feel obliged to let Regina know about it before we made any sort of commitment. This isn't any different."

My throat felt tight, and my eyes burned. I would have been crying, except that tears are one of the things I lost when I turned into a part-time wolf. Even now, I don't know how much of my anger came from what Dad obviously thought was the primary source—resentment of a possible rival—how much was sheer panic at the thought of having my secret come out, and how much was something more. Something I'd just discovered.

"You really do think it's something like—like being crippled, or blind, or crazy. A—a disability. A *handicap*."

"Valerie—"

"You don't know," I said. "You don't know anything about it at all."

After that, neither of us said anything much for the rest of the meal. I still don't remember what I had for dessert that night.

When it was over, we got into the car and drove back home, not talking. The digital clock on the dashboard read 10:37—late for a school night. At least I'd finished my homework before we left for dinner; as soon as we got back to the house, I could fall into bed and try to get some sleep.

We were halfway home, and going right at the speed limit, when a black BMW zoomed past us like we were standing still.

My dad said, "I hope he gets where he's going"—sounding irritated and glad of the distraction at the same time.

I didn't say anything. I wasn't sulking, or at least not much; I was too preoccupied with what I had seen as the BMW flashed by. The interior of the other car had been too dark to see clearly, even with the lights along the highway, but I could have sworn the person on the passenger side was Elise Barbizon.

Can't be, I thought. *It's a school night.*

But the more I thought about it, the more certain I got. The rider in the BMW, a pale, fair-haired girl with a face caught in some odd emotion halfway between pleasure and fear—the rider had been Elise.

About the driver I couldn't be sure. The shadows had been too deep. But I thought he might be older than Elise, just from his posture and profile. There certainly wasn't anybody at Hillside High with a car like that.

The whole thing worried me, for some reason. That odd, frightened-but-not-frightened expression on Elise's face got into the back of my mind and stayed there. I had bad dreams all night long—disturbing nightmares full of blood and strange voices calling in the dark—and I still felt tired when I woke up.

Elise was at school the next day, which was a bit of a relief. She didn't look good, though; she was paler than ever, and her eyes looked like she hadn't slept for a week.

We didn't have a chance to talk until lunchtime, because most of the morning was taken up by a pep rally for this week's football game. By the time we'd settled down at one of the wobbly folding tables, me with my double cheeseburger and Elise with a plate of salad that looked even limper and more washed-out than she did, I was starting to get really worried. She wasn't well, no matter what she tried to tell me; and if she was running around behind her parents' backs with the kind of older men who drove shiny black sports cars way above the speed limit, then she was headed for serious trouble.

It had already occurred to me that the two problems might be connected—I didn't spend *all* my time in health education class wondering if werewolves got fleas. So I may have sounded a bit sharper than I meant to when I asked, "Hey, who was that guy in the BMW?"

"What guy?" she asked, wide-eyed.

53

"The one I saw you with last night, out on the highway."

She shook her head. "What do you mean? I didn't go anywhere last night."

"Funny," I said. "I could have sworn it was you. Unless you've got a long-lost twin sister—"

"That must be it," she said. "Because I was home all evening."

I wasn't certain I believed her, but I didn't want to say so. I finished up my cheeseburger and watched Elise move bits of lettuce around with her fork. After a while I said, "I'm home by myself tonight, believe it or not—no date for the game, and my dad's got a new girlfriend. Do you want to come over and watch TV or something?"

"No," she said. "I can't leave the house."

Grounded again after last night? I wanted to say. But instead I said, "Maybe I could come over to your place?"

"No," she said again. "That wouldn't work. I'm going to try to catch up on my sleep. I've been tired a lot lately."

"I kind of noticed," I said. "Elise, are you sure you're doing okay? Maybe you really ought to see a doctor—"

"Just let me alone," she said, not even sounding angry, just sort of flat and worn-out. "I don't want to talk about it anymore, all right?"

She picked up her mostly untouched salad and left. I was all alone with my french fries and a carton of milk, wondering just how much I was supposed to worry about someone I'd only known since last summer. After all, I wasn't Elise Barbizon's mother. But she was what passed for my best female friend, which had to mean something. I stared at my milk carton and thought about bad things, like why Elise's parents couldn't think of anything to do about her problems—whatever they were—except for ordering her to stay home.

Thinking about homes and parents made me think of mine, and about this Regina Polidori person whom I'd never met. I wasn't afraid of hating her. I knew Dad well enough to be sure he wouldn't marry anybody I absolutely couldn't stand. But I didn't like the idea of somebody else moving in on a part of my life—with some gourmet person around the house would I even be allowed to make a quick-and-dirty meat loaf anymore? Or would I be kicked out of the kitchen, and would we always have fancy things with French names?

I sat and brooded. I didn't have a chance to brood for long, though. Freddie Hanger, of all people, showed up to join me.

"Val," he said. "We've got to talk."

"Not now," I said. If he'd finally made up his mind to ask me out, he'd picked the wrong time to do it. After last night, I was feeling burnt-out on the whole idea of dating and romance.

"Now," he said. "Didn't you listen to the radio this morning?"

"No. Why?"

He was looking grim. "Because there's another missing kid out there. And this time they found the body."

I had a feeling I wasn't going to like what came next. "And?"

"The cops are calling it an animal attack. Sound familiar?"

It did, of course. "Animal attack" was what the police had called it back when my fellow lycanthrope, unfriend, and all-around menace to society, Jay Collins, was making his mark on the neighborhood.

"Sorry, wrong person," I said. "No full moon last night, remember? I spent the evening out at the Carson House with my dad."

"Yeah," he said. "But not everything that isn't a real animal has to be a you-know-what."

"You can say it," I said. "Werewolf."

"Okay. Werewolf." Freddie looked sheepish but determined. "I know you don't like to talk about it, but I need to know if you, well, *noticed* anything the last time you were, uh, out."

I thought about that for a while. "Freddie, there's something out there—I've been feeling it around. But I don't know what it is, and I don't want to find out. Dealing with Jay was bad enough."

He gave me the same kind of doubtful look I'd just given Elise. "All right," he said. "But let me know if you change your mind, okay? Because if what you've noticed is what I think it is, we're all in big trouble."

"Let's quit dancing around the question. What do you think is out there?"

"Vampires."

I stared at him. "You're kidding."

"No," he said. "It's . . . they've been going after the livestock since the middle of summer. All nights of the month."

"You never said anything about that before."

"You never asked. Anyhow, my dad still thinks it's coyotes, or maybe a mountain lion down from the hills."

"None of those around here," I said automatically. "I'd have—" I paused, then went on. "I'd have smelled them by now."

"That's what I thought," he said. "So if we rule out natural predators, that leaves unnatural predators. And they've moved on to bigger game than sheep."

Chapter
Six

I THOUGHT about what Freddie had said for a minute. Like a lot of his ideas, it felt uncomfortable, like an inconvenient truth. Freddie's a great one for being the first to notice that the roof you spent all summer repairing has just sprung three new leaks. But before I could ask the next question—*"If there really is a vampire out there, what are we supposed to do about it?"*—the bell rang for the end of lunch period and it was off to French class for me and the computer lab for Freddie.

I was hoping to catch him after school for some more talk, but by the time I got down to the parking lot his rusty old pickup was already pulling away. So I shrugged and caught the bus home.

Most of the afternoon I spent fiddling around the house, dusting and polishing mirrors and things like that. Dad and I share those chores, too, and once a week someone comes in from a local housecleaning service. That was Dad's idea, after Grandmother moved to Florida; he said that if I was going to school full-time, and he was working full-time, we deserved a bit of professional assistance with the heavy stuff. I wondered how much of that would change if Dad's hopes worked out.

By the time he left for his date with Ms. Polidori, I was feeling pretty glum. I watched him go out the door, then settled down at the kitchen table with the homework I'd been putting off all afternoon.

If you really work at it, you can make an hour's worth of school assignments stretch out to take all evening. I worked at it—which is how I happened to still be up when my father came home. He gave me a kind of suspicious glance—I don't usually need until 11:30 P.M. to finish my homework, especially on a Friday night—but he didn't say anything.

I started putting away my books and papers. "Nice date?" I asked.

"I've had worse," he said, but I could tell from his voice that he was pleased with the way things were going. "You'll be glad to know that Regina agrees with you about the steak tartare."

"Oh, good," I said. I wondered how things had gone for him and Ms. Polidori after dinner—but the thought of a couple of grown-ups going out parking was weird enough that I didn't want to dwell on it for very long. "Are you going to ask her out again soon?"

"Actually," he said; "I was thinking of having Regina and her brother over for dinner this weekend."

"You're cooking, right?" No way I was going to put a meat loaf, or even my struggling-student taco casserole, on the table in front of somebody who ran her own catering service.

"I'm cooking," Dad agreed. "If I can't impress her in the kitchen, maybe I can get away with evoking pity."

We both laughed at that—my laughter was nine-tenths relief, but I hoped it didn't show—and I went off to bed.

Sunday was the day of the dinner party. In spite of the fact that the house was already as clean as the housekeeping service could get it, we spent most of Saturday cleaning it some more. I even had to clean out the closet in my room, for heaven's sake! I felt like asking Dad if he was planning to introduce Regina Polidori to my coat hanger collection, but something told me it wouldn't be a good idea.

By Sunday afternoon, everything was starched and polished and as ready as it was going to get. I put on a good school dress—one of the ones I wear when there's some reason I can't just go with any of my usual jeans-and-sweater outfits—and then I sat in the kitchen, waiting. I might have enjoyed watching Dad get more and more nervous as the clock hands circled on toward evening, if I hadn't been so twitchy myself.

61

As it turned out, Regina showed up early. There was a knocking on the front door, and Dad was out of his chair and on the way to answer the knock before I could even open my mouth to say, "I'll get it."

There was the sound of voices in the entryway, and then Dad came back into the kitchen. Regina Polidori was with him.

The co-owner of the Clever Gourmet—my dad's girlfriend—was a petite woman with dark hair and a ruffled blouse. She wore a cameo pinned at her neck on a black velvet ribbon. Somewhat to my surprise, she looked as nervous as Dad and I had been, and the smile she turned in my direction was almost shy.

Think about it, Teen Wonder. For all she knows, you're auditioning her for the role of Wicked Stepmother in a live-action Really Grim Fairy Tale.

"Hello, Valerie." Regina Polidori had a pleasant, rather husky alto voice. "I've been looking forward to meeting you."

Your boyfriend's werewolf daughter . . . I'll bet you have. I wondered how much Dad had told her about me already.

I glanced over at him, but he didn't look like his conscience was bothering him about anything—and if he'd felt obliged to Tell All to Ms. Polidori in the name of honest relationships, he'd better have been feeling guilty the whole time about violating *my* confidence.

So I smiled at Regina while Dad made the formal introductions. He looked relieved, which made me wonder what he'd been expecting me to do. Let me tell you, it's touching when your relatives show so much confidence in your good behavior.

After that—well, we made dinner. Dad had bought all the stuff we needed the day before, and the way things worked out, all three of us wound up doing the cooking. A bit to my surprise, I found myself telling Regina about my "garlic allergy" and how embarrassing it could be if I wasn't careful, and about the way my grandmother taught me to make meat loaf— "She always used oatmeal to bind it together; she thought bread crumbs made it too stodgy"—and about the food service lunches at school, where mystery meat was a way of life.

"That's the problem with institutional cooking," Regina said. We were sitting around the kitchen table by then, drinking Cokes and waiting for everything to finish cooking. I was glad to find out that she wasn't the sort of fancy-food person who only drinks funny-tasting mineral water. "Whoever's planning the meals has to serve too many masters."

"What do you mean?" I said.

"It's not just the people with allergies like yours," she said. "It's them; and it's the people who think that 'nasty foreign stuff' means dishes seasoned with anything besides salt, pepper, and margarine; and it's the other people who want to make certain that you follow all the current healthy-food guidelines; and the *other* people who want to make certain that whatever you do, you don't spend too much of the institution's money while you're doing it. . . . When you think about it, it's surprising that anything edible comes out of the kitchen at all."

Dad laughed. "You sound like you speak from experience."

"I do," she told him. "I did institutional cooking for five years back on the East Coast before Jonathan and I decided to strike out on our own with the Clever Gourmet."

So Dad's girlfriend is a refugee from a school lunchroom.

The idea cheered me up a lot. Somehow, it helped to make Regina Polidori less intimidating. There was still her brother to meet, but he wasn't a candidate for live-in family member status the way Regina was.

In the end, Jonathan Polidori didn't make it to the dinner after all. At almost the last minute, Regina got a phone call from him. There had been some sort of mix-up at the shop—Sunday afternoon, it seemed, was the time they usually spent getting ready for the Monday rush—and he was going to have to stay late to take care of it. He'd try to stop by the house afterward, Regina said, in order to meet Dad and me.

So we ate our meal without him, which didn't bother me any. It didn't bother Dad and Regina, either, if you ask me. We'd finished the dessert and were loading plates into the dishwasher before there was another knock on the front door. Dad answered it again, and came back this time with Jonathan Polidori.

I didn't like Regina's brother at all, even on the first meeting. He was a smallish man, no taller than his sister but quite a bit more muscular, and very neatly dressed—"dapper" was the word that came instantly to mind—with smooth black hair and a thin black mustache. And a bit of the wolf was still in me, no matter whether the moon was full or not—because all I had to do was look at Mr. Polidori and I could feel the hair rise on the back of my neck. It was all I could do to keep from growling.

Down, girl, I told myself. Life was interesting enough without biting my future step-uncle on the ankle to add to the thrills. Even if he did smell overpoweringly of Lysol—apparently the trouble at the shop had involved heavy cleanup duty on top of everything else.

He wasn't in a very social mood, either. Dad offered him a drink, but he shook his head no.

"I have more work left to do tonight," he said. His accent was some kind of East Coast ethnic thing, a lot stronger than Regina's. "I need to have all my wits about me."

Then Regina began to get flustered, saying that she needed to get back to the shop herself, she'd taken too much time off. Jonathan didn't look satisfied. He started trying to talk Regina into going back to the shop right then, with him.

"I will need your help," he said, "if I am to finish everything by tomorrow morning."

Regina gave Dad a helpless "I know he's being a pain, but he's family" kind of look, and stood up to put on her jacket. Dad's face was a sight. He was obviously trying for an understanding "It's been a great evening anyhow" expression— but it kept getting mixed up with the stiff, disapproving face he keeps for men who try to make doormats out of the other people in their lives. Jonathan Polidori, it was obvious, fit firmly into that last category.

After the Polidoris had left, Dad sat down in one of the kitchen chairs and said, "Well."

"Well," I said. "*She's* okay."

His face brightened. "You really think so?"

"Would I lie to you? Her brother's a bit of a jerk, though."

He sighed. "I wouldn't have put it in quite those terms—but it's immaterial, in any case. People can't choose the relatives they're born with."

I couldn't help it. "Just the ones they marry later?"

Dad turned red. "We haven't discussed anything like that yet, Val."

The "yet" was a dead giveaway, of course, but I decided not to push it. I wasn't quite ready to be bosom buddies with Regina Polidori, but as Wicked Stepmothers went she probably wouldn't be too bad. Just as long as Brother Jonathan didn't hang around too much—and from the way Dad had looked at him, that wouldn't be a problem.

Aside from the dinner party, nothing much happened all weekend. I finished reading the book that Elise had loaned me, and I got a long letter from my old junior high school friend Diana, off at her private boarding school. The letter sounded like she was getting real tired of life back East. I was kind of glad; maybe if she got tired enough, she could convince her folks to let her come back to Hillside High.

Monday I went back to school, carrying Elise's book with me to return it to her, but she wasn't there. She wasn't in school on Tuesday, either, and when I phoned her house, nobody answered.

On Wednesday, Elise still wasn't back in school. And Freddie Hanger grabbed me by the sleeve in the hallway between chem class and history. "Things are worse," he said. "Now we *really* have to talk."

I didn't have time to ask what he meant; I had to hurry to get to my next class. Freddie was serious about wanting to talk, though. After school he was waiting down by the bus stop in his old pickup.

"Let me give you a ride home, okay?" he said.

I couldn't think of a way to say no—and besides, with Elise out of school I hadn't really had anybody to talk to for almost a week. Except my dad, of course, but that's not the same thing.

Freddie opened the passenger-side door and I climbed in. "We really need to talk," he said again.

"I figured. My house is on the other side of town from your family's place."

"It isn't that far," he said. "I've driven there once or twice—giving you a lift won't make me late getting home."

"Okay," I said. "We can talk on the way. But I've got homework to do, so don't expect me to ask you in for milk and cookies."

"That's what I wanted to talk about," Freddie said as we pulled away from the curb. "Don't trust me. Don't trust anyone. If someone comes up to your door and asks to be invited inside— even if it's your best friend—even if it's Elise— don't say, 'Hey, come on in.'"

"I can't just go slamming my door in somebody's face."

"It might not be a bad idea."

"Sure," I said. "Make enemies out of the two or three people who actually bother to come visit me once in a while."

He didn't say anything. When I glanced over at him, I noticed that he had the pickup's rearview mirror set so that he could see whoever was riding in the passenger seat at the same time as he watched the road. It made me wonder exactly what kind of passengers he was expecting.

"You never used to be this paranoid," I said, after a minute or two. "What happened?"

"It started during the summer," he said. "But I didn't start putting all the pieces together until the past few weeks."

"So tell me about it."

"Last July," he said, "somebody knocked on *my* door just as the sun went below the horizon."

"You're awfully exact about that."

"I could see it," he said. "The door faces west. We'd had rain all afternoon, and the bottoms of the clouds were red. And this elderly guy in a grey business suit shows up at the front door, wanting to know if he could come in to use the phone."

"That line's been around ever since Alexander Graham Bell hung up on Watson," I said. "Don't tell me you fell for it."

"I didn't. I told him, 'Hey, who do you want to call? I can take a message for you.'"

Freddie paused. "So then this guy looks at me, right into my eyes, and says, 'Invite me in,' like all he had to do was say it, and I'd do anything he wanted. He was almost right, too—I *wanted* to ask him in. Just looking at him, I could practically feel the words in my throat. I might have said them, too, except that I suddenly realized that, hey, here was this guy standing on my front step and he didn't have a car anywhere in sight."

"He could have walked," I said.

"Out to a farm? In a three-piece suit? It'd been raining hard—we had water and mud all over— and this guy didn't have a drop on him."

"So what happened?"

"So I said, *'In nomine Christi exorcio te, creatura nocturnalis,'* and slammed the door in his face."

69

Chapter
Seven

I STARED at him. " '*In nomine*'—what's that?"

"Latin. It's an exorcism."

"I can tell you've been watching too many cruddy horror flicks. Since when did you know Latin?"

Mentioning horror movies made me think of our friend Bill, even though it had been over a year since Bill had died—since Jay Collins had killed him on his way home from a sneak preview—and I felt rotten. I think I reminded Freddie, too. His voice, when he answered, was sharper than usual.

"After what happened last year, I figured the odds. If one thing is real, why not everything? So I decided to get myself prepared. I cast more of those silver bullets. . . ."

I winced. "Don't remind me. My side still aches sometimes."

He looked defensive. "I've practiced a lot since then. I've got a row of garlic growing in the garden. . . ."

"Ick." Just the thought of garlic made my stomach do flip-flops. "And I bet you've got a pile of crosses and stakes and mallets in your bedroom, and a couple of torches out by the pitchforks in the barn."

"How did you know? Yeah, and a kris and a bottle of lime juice, too."

"A kris and lime juice? What on earth for?"

"In case of *berbalangs*," he said, in a tone of voice that said he thought I'd gone simpleminded. "Malaysian zombies. They're invisible."

"Freddie, I'm prepared to believe in a lot of things, but invisible zombies?"

"Why not?"

"Right," I said. "How about aluminum foil hats to keep out the Martian thought-control rays?" He gave me a dirty look, and I went on. "So anyway, what happened after you gabbled some Latin at this guy and shut the door?"

"Nothing," he said. "When I looked out through the side window, I didn't see anybody on the porch. There weren't any footprints, either. And I never saw him again."

"Suppose he ran off? Suppose it was just some banker with a broken-down car that you scared out of a month's growth?"

Freddie looked stubborn. My grandmother always used to say he was the second most pigheaded person she knew. "I already told you there wasn't any car. Or any footprints. Come on, Val. What shows up after sunset, doesn't leave tracks, and can't come in unless you invite it? He was a vampire."

Everything Freddie had said sounded like something I'd already thought. If there are werewolves, then why not Bigfoot, the Loch Ness Monster, vampires, ghosts, and everything else?

But you can't believe all that at once or you'll go crazy, assuming you weren't already. For myself, I've gotten used to the idea of lycanthropy mostly because I've never seen anything supernatural about it. I mean, *I'm* a lycanthrope, and I know darned well there's nothing supernatural about *me*.

"A vampire," I said, and waited for Freddie to go on.

"I've been researching this stuff," he said. "As far as I can tell, there aren't any real experts. So that makes me as good as anyone else. And I've been thinking about a lot of things."

"No kidding. Like what?"

"Like Jay—where did he come from? What made him like that?"

"Jay was born mean," I said, "and his father's an asshole. So he grew up into a mean asshole. Turning into a wolf just gave him a few more choices on how to express himself."

"Some people," said Freddie, "say that when a werewolf dies he turns into a vampire."

I'd read those same books. The thought didn't cheer me any. But most of what I'd read about werewolves was nonsense anyway—and if I was going to start turning into a supernatural crea-

73

ture of evil I hadn't noticed the changes yet. Not that I didn't worry about it sometimes. But I wasn't about to let Freddie in on my private nightmares.

"Some people are fruitcakes," I said. "When a werewolf dies, he turns into a dead werewolf. Period."

"How do you know? Maybe whoever made Jay—what he was—died last summer, came back as a vampire, and decided to see how his fair-haired boy was doing."

"You're just saying that to cheer me up," I said.

Freddie ignored me. "And some of the other books claim that vampires control lycanthropes— use them to run errands in daylight, that sort of stuff. Maybe that's what somebody wanted Jay for, and they saw to it that he got turned. Now he's dead, and they're mad."

"Mmh," I said. Much as I didn't like the idea, I had to admit that Jay would have made the perfect sidekick for a nocturnal bloodsucker. " 'They'? A minute ago it was just one guy in a business suit. What's this 'they' routine?"

"Because we don't know there's only one vampire."

"*We* don't know there are *any*."

"I do," Freddie said. "I keep my eyes open these days, and I've seen things. So far we've got two kids vanished without a trace—"

"Two kids? I only heard of one."

"You should listen to the news more often.
Two. Plus the one that they're blaming on 'wild
animals.' And then there's your friend Elise."

I have to admit, I got a sinking feeling when I
thought about Elise. My worries had been more
along the lines of family troubles and eating dis-
orders—I'm a psychiatrist's daughter, after all—
but once you bit the silver bullet and assumed
vampires, Freddie's hypothesis worked too well
for comfort.

"Elise," I said. "Tell me what you think about
Elise."

"She was perfectly normal-looking when school
started," Freddie said. "A bit on the skinny side,
but okay—not like a famine victim with a sleep
deficit, which is what she looked like by this time
last week. And she was wearing high collars and
scarves or turtleneck sweaters every day for a
solid month."

"That's not a crime."

"No, but maybe it's evidence. Think about it,
Val. She was away from home all night one
night—"

"With Steve Barnett. You're not going to tell
me *he's* a vampire, are you?"

"No. But he isn't the last of the red-hot lov-
ers, either, and Steve says he dropped her off at
home before eleven."

"He could be lying."

"That's not the sort of lie guys tell. If he was
saying, 'Yeah, we did it,' and she was saying,
'No,' then I'd say he was fibbing. Trust me—I'm

a guy. Guys don't lie about *not* doing something like that."

"It figures," I said.

Freddie ignored me. "Elise wasn't the first girl at Hillside to turn pale and switch to high collars, either. There was a senior, about a month before Elise developed dark circles under her eyes—and *she* hasn't been back in school since the day before the Johnson kid disappeared."

"Sometimes people who get sick don't come back," I pointed out. "Better be careful asking questions about things like that. Depending on what exactly was wrong with that girl, you might get her folks mad at you."

"I'm not real worried about what somebody's parents think," Freddie said. "There's bad stuff out there."

We'd reached my street by now, so Freddie pulled over to drop me off. And, as usual, he had to have the last word.

"I used to think that vampires didn't exist," he said, as I opened the passenger-side door and hopped down. "But now I'm pretty sure they do. And if they do, and if I'm the only person who believes it, then it's my responsibility to do something about them—isn't it?"

"Okay," I said, "I'm thinking about it. But before you go out hunting with a hammer and stake, call me this time, okay?"

"Yeah," he said, and drove off.

I stood there watching until the pickup was out of sight. It was getting late in the year—

the November full moon was only a couple of days away—and the sun was low in the sky. A wind blew out of the north. Then, for the first time, I remembered the dream I'd had that night Freddie and I had gone to the movies with Elise and Steve Barnett. I'd stood on the doorstep, shivering, just like I was now, and a strange man in a grey suit had asked me to let him in—

—and I'd said yes.

It was a dream, I told myself. But the voice in the back of my head that sometimes can talk sense into me said, *Are you really sure?*

I shivered again and ran into the house.

Dad came home a couple of hours later, just as I was finishing my homework. I closed my book and looked up. "Hi, Dad. You're home a bit late tonight."

"I had some paperwork to finish," he said. "I decided to do it at the office instead of bringing it home. Why spoil the rest of the evening that way?"

"You've got a point there," I said. "I feel the same way about homework sometimes."

My assignments for tonight were all done, though, and I was—not surprisingly—hungry again, so I started to make myself a peanut butter and jelly sandwich for a snack. I was just fitting the pieces of bread together and getting ready to slice the whole thing in half when someone knocked on the door.

"I'll get it," Dad said, before I could put down the knife. He was out of the room in half a second, leaving me standing there with a sandwich in front of me and a sinking feeling in the pit of my stomach—because just a moment before the knock sounded the sun had dipped below the horizon.

My dad was back a minute later. "Visitor for you," he said. "She's in the living room. Want to go talk with her?"

Uh-oh, I thought. For some reason, I was convinced that my after-dark visitor was going to be Ms. Polidori. But when I went into the living room, all I saw was Elise Barbizon, sitting on the couch and leafing through an old copy of *National Geographic*.

"What are you doing here?" I said. I could probably have said it better—my grandmother would never have put up with something that rude— but I'd just been discussing her with Freddie, not to mention expecting to see somebody else altogether.

"I said I wanted to talk with you," Elise said, "and your father asked me in." She paused, then giggled. "He invited me."

I felt a trickle of cold sweat run down my spine. She was probably just talking ... but I couldn't help remembering Freddie's story about the mysterious stranger who hadn't left footprints. And whatever had kept Elise in turtleneck sweaters for the past month wasn't bothering her anymore, either; she was wearing a white, man-tailored blouse with an open collar.

I sat down at the other end of the couch, near the door. I wasn't afraid, exactly—lycanthrope strength and speed would give me an edge no matter what happened—just lots more alert than usual.

"So what did you come here for, anyway?"

Elise glanced out the window. It gets dark fast in November after the sun goes down.

"There are things going on," she said. "I'm scared."

I believed it: her eyes were big and dark, and her laughter a moment before had sounded as much like nerves as humor. So I leaned back against the upholstery and tried to look nonthreatening, the way Dad does when he's in professional listening mode.

"What are you scared of?" I asked.

Elise looked at me. "I don't want to be dead."

I didn't like the way this was going, not at all. I took a deep breath and said, cautiously, "Who does?"

"I did," Elise said.

Damn, I thought. I started rearranging my theories again. *Suicide attempt? Is that why she looked so bad last week—was she getting over a dose of pills?*

I was starting to wonder if maybe I ought to excuse myself, go to the kitchen for a Coke, and have a quick chat with Dad along the way. Instead, I stayed where I was.

"Why would you want something like that?" I asked.

"It sounded so neat," Elise said. "All the power and everything. But it turned out different. There are things you wouldn't understand. . . ."

This was *not* sounding like a suicide attempt. I tried to keep looking casual. "Try me."

"The worst of it is the cold, and being hungry all the time. You know how you're always eating and making a joke out of it? And how you thought I wasn't eating enough? I wasn't hungry then, but I am now."

"Hungry for what?"

She looked away, not meeting my eyes. "Can't tell."

The floor lamp wasn't doing much to cut the gloom. I reached out to switch on the lamp beside the couch.

"No, don't do that," Elise said. "I'm here to say, well, good-bye, and I wanted to say it to you—"

That did it. "Excuse me," I said, standing up. "I think I'd like to get a Coke. You want one, too?"

"I don't drink—Coke," Elise said, and laughed again, that same nervous giggle. The sound of it froze me where I stood.

"Look," I said hastily. "Let's not talk about saying good-bye. I'll see you in school tomorrow, right?"

"I don't think so," Elise said. "I thought I could go on the same as before, but it turns out not to be as easy as I'd thought, as easy as he'd said."

"Who's he?"

"My . . . friend."

"Your friend?" I thought about the half-glimpsed stranger I'd seen with Elise the other night. "Who is he? Are you in trouble?"

"Oh, no, all my troubles are over. So to speak. You don't know him, but he knows about you, Val. Be careful. Please."

"I'm always careful," I said. "I try to be, anyhow. So what can I do for you?"

"Nothing. Set me free, maybe. No, there's nothing you can do." She was talking wildly, contradicting herself; her eyes were all pupil, dark and afraid. "Val, help me."

I don't know what I might have said. At that moment another knock sounded on the front door. I heard Dad call, "I'll get it!" from the kitchen, and then I heard his footsteps going down the hall. A moment later came the sound of a door opening, and Dad saying cheerfully, "Come in!"

Another moment, and they were both at the door to the living room: my dad and Regina Polidori. As upset about Elise as I was, I felt a brief stirring of hostility: *talk about your standing invitations to come and visit . . . she already thinks she can just drop in anytime she wants to.*

But I stood up anyway—Grandmother raised me properly and sometimes the training stuck—and my dad said, "Kids, Regina and I are planning to go out for dinner in a little—hmm. Where did your friend run off to, Val?"

I turned back around. Elise was gone. And the only door to the living room was the one my father was standing in.

Chapter
Eight

ELISE HADN'T left any trace she'd been there, either. Not even a depression on the couch cushions. I swallowed hard.

"Uh . . . Elise left, I guess." Then, before Dad could ask me where she'd gone (and what the heck was I going to tell him if he did?), I said, "Excuse me, I have to go call a school friend about some homework. Dad, can we talk later?"

"Sure, Val, anytime."

"Thanks." I edged past them into the hallway. "Bye, Ms. Polidori. Nice seeing you."

I went to the extension phone in the kitchen—no way was I going to use the living room phone—and punched in Freddie's number. I had to look it up in the phone book first. Freddie wasn't somebody like Di or Elise had been, that I'd call up sometimes just to chat.

The phone rang at the other end, then stopped as someone picked it up.

It was Freddie's mother. "Hello?"

"Hi, this is Val Sherwood—is Freddie there?"

Freddie's mother is nice; I've met her a few times. "Hello, Valerie," she said. "No, I'm afraid Freddie isn't here right now. Can I take a message?"

"Just tell him to please call me back when he can. It's about something we talked about today." I paused. "Tell him he was right."

After I'd hung up the telephone, I stayed in the kitchen for a while, finishing up the sandwich I'd been making when Elise came knocking at the door. In spite of everything that had happened this afternoon, I was still hungry.

After I'd eaten the sandwich, I walked back to the living room. Dad and Ms. Polidori were sitting on the couch and talking. Simply by looking at them, I could tell that they were already a bit more than just good friends; for one thing, I'd spotted Regina holding Dad's hand when I came through the door. I pretended I didn't notice.

"Hi," Dad said. "What's up?"

"Hey, Dad, can I have the car keys? I have to go meet Freddie—we're working on a project together, and we have to do some planning if we want to get it finished."

He looked dubious. "Isn't this all rather last-minute? Regina and I were planning to go out ourselves."

Ms. Polidori squeezed his hand. "It's all right. We can take my car."

"Since it's for schoolwork . . . I suppose so." He pulled the keys out of his pocket and tossed them over to me. "Be back by nine, okay? This is a school night."

"Sure thing," I said, checking my watch. It was a few minutes after five. Four hours. I could get a lot done in four hours. "See you later, Dad, Ms. Polidori. I've got to run."

I grabbed my jacket on the way out the front door—it's downright cold outside on a November evening—and went to the car. Another time I might have felt pleased that Dad had trusted me to handle it by myself at night, with the new barely worn off of my license after taking summer-school driver's ed. Right now, though, I had other things on my mind.

Overhead, the sky was the dark blue of twilight in winter, fading to black and already thick with stars. The moon would come up soon—I could feel it calling to me. Not long until it was full again.

It wasn't until I was well on my way that I wondered where I thought I was going. To find vampires? I growled under my breath and set the radio to a rock station, turned up loud.

The music didn't help my mood any, unfortunately. I kept on thinking about what Freddie had said earlier that afternoon, and about Elise. *The only two friends I've got at Hillside High*, I thought gloomily, *and one of them is accusing the other of being a supernatural creature of evil.*

And the bad part is, I'm starting to believe it.

I didn't have proof. Not real proof. I wanted

85

to know for sure. There was only one person who could tell me whether Freddie had been right about Elise Barbizon—and that was Elise herself. If she'd gone over to being a vampire, I wanted to find out how she'd been keeping the news from her parents.

I knew where she lived: a plain brick ranch-style house with a neatly kept front yard, not too far away from the school. When I got there, all the windows were dark, even though it was still early and lights were showing in all the other houses up and down the street.

I parked across the street from the house. Then I sat in the car for a while, feeling really, really stupid. What was I going to do now? Knock on the door and say, "Excuse me, Mr. and Mrs. Barbizon, you don't know me, but I think your daughter is one of the undead, and have you noticed if she's been sleeping in a coffin lately?"

I almost felt stupid enough to start the car and get going again, but I didn't. Instead I started worrying about the darkened house across the street from me. If all the lights were out, why was the car in the driveway?

Finally I pulled the emergency flashlight out of the glove compartment, put it in my jacket pocket, and walked across the street to the Barbizons' front door. I rang the bell, then knocked—first softly, then harder. Nobody came.

I twisted the doorknob. It was unlocked.

I swallowed. "I have to be crazy."

I pushed the door all the way open and went

inside. Then I pulled out my flashlight and looked around.

It sure didn't seem like anybody was home. But I could pick up an odd and disquieting smell on the still air, unsettling and vaguely familiar, and under it the odor of something else, something buried and recently dug up. After a moment, I recognized the dead-and-rotting smell that had disturbed me on the night of the last full moon. Elsewhere in the house a faint, indistinct noise went on in a continuous undertone.

TV, probably. The family room would be in the back. Did the television mean that someone was home after all, and just hadn't heard the doorbell—or had they all gone off somewhere, leaving the car in the driveway and the TV on? I told myself that I was making the worst mistake of my life, but even that didn't make me turn around and leave.

The beam of my flashlight shone into dark corners and open doors, lighting up here a piano, there a side table with a stack of stamped and addressed letters waiting to be put in the mail. I kept walking toward the sound.

A door opened off the hall. I looked. It was the guest bathroom, with neatly folded monogrammed towels hanging over the polished brass rack. The silver-backed mirror over the sink had been smashed—hit so many times with something hard and heavy that the frame was empty and the sink beneath it was full of broken glass.

I don't like this, I thought, but I kept on going.

At last I came to the room where the TV still played, its voice a low mutter and its pallid light flickering. The smell I'd noticed before was all over everything now. I felt the hair rise up on the back of my neck.

I wanted to leave, but I couldn't. I had to find out—I had to talk with Elise. I stepped into the room, flashlight shining ahead of me, and then halted.

Two middle-aged people sat on the couch, staring with wide, unblinking eyes at the moving pictures on the television screen. They were dead, their necks twisted at unnatural angles, and the fronts of their clothes stained with dried blood.

For a few seconds, all I could do was stand there. I'd seen some ugly stuff before, the night that my friend Greg got his throat torn out by Jay Collins in wolf-shape and Di had blown Jay's brains out with a .45—but I'd been in wolf-shape myself at the time, and somehow the violence and the sight and smell of blood hadn't bothered me as much. But now I was in human form, and I felt the bile rising in my throat.

I'd come here to find out how my friend Elise could be a vampire without her parents knowing. It looked like I'd just found out.

I backed out of the room one step at a time. I should have gotten out of the house completely— it would have been the smart thing to do—but I still hadn't found Elise. I'm not sure why I wasn't more afraid of meeting her, especially after what I'd just seen in the TV room. Part of it came from knowing something she didn't: that I wasn't an

ordinary one-shaped human, that I had lycanthropic strength and speed and stamina to call
on if I needed to. But most of it, I think, came
from remembering that she'd asked me for help.

I looked through the bedrooms next. I didn't
have any trouble figuring out which one belonged to Elise. It had posters on the walls,
stuffed animals on the bed, and ruffles on the
curtains. A typical girl's room, right out of the
catalogue—if you didn't count the mirror, broken
into pieces just like the one in the bathroom. I
walked in and flashed the light around. Empty.

Then I saw someone lying on the bed.

It was Elise. I hadn't noticed her before. Maybe
she hadn't been there when I came in; maybe
she'd clouded my mind. Who knows? But her
eyes were open and unblinking like a china
doll's, and she was looking straight at me.

She sat up—all in one smooth motion, without
apparent effort, bending at the waist like she
was made of wood and had a hinge in there. It
was the most unhuman thing I'd ever seen anyone do, and it convinced me of what she was, like
nothing else could have. I still wonder, sometimes, if that was why she did it.

"Hello, Val," she said. "I was hoping you'd
come."

"I'm here," I said. I didn't want to say what I
said next, but I had to have the answer. "Elise,
who killed your parents?"

She took a minute before she answered. "I did.
He did. He wanted me to do it." Her eyes got wide

and dark again, like they had when she'd asked me to help her. "Oh, Val, I didn't want to!"

"I believe you," I said. But I had a cold feeling right under my breastbone. This was Elise. She'd been my friend. She wasn't like Jay Collins, who'd been bad all along. She'd made a choice, and now she was trapped in it. That was worse, maybe, than being born bad; but I could hate Jay with a clear conscience, and I still couldn't hate Elise.

I swallowed hard. "What are you going to do?"

"Kill more people and drink their blood," Elise said. The way she said it was so matter-of-fact that it made me think, sickeningly, of the rabbits that I'd caught and eaten on full-moon nights. "I have to."

"Elise," I said, "nobody *has* to do anything."

"Does it even matter?" asked Elise, but not like she was gloating. She mostly sounded tired. "He's everywhere, and we can't do anything against his will."

That "he," again. I thought of the older man in the BMW, the man in the grey suit who'd shown up on Freddie's doorstep—and later, on mine. The connection wasn't hard to make.

"So being a vampire didn't turn out to be as much fun as your friend in the fancy car promised you it would?"

"My *friend*." Her face contorted in a snarl. I could see the fangs glisten briefly before her lips covered them again. "He lied to me about everything. You have to stop him, Val."

Right. Stop a master vampire. Nothing to it.

That made me think of Freddie, with his stakes and mallets and backyard garlic garden. Two days ago I wouldn't have believed a word Freddie had to say about all this. And here I was, talking about it with a living corpse.

A corpse. But Elise is still in there. What does it feel like, walking around inside a dead body?

I shoved that idea into the back of my head real fast, because it was giving me the shakes, and went back to the problem at hand. "This guy isn't God, is he? So tell me his name. Tell me where he lives."

"Lives." She made a noise that wasn't quite a laugh. "Funny you should use that word."

"You know what I mean. Who is he?"

"Call him Mr. Grey. That's what I called him." She made that noise again. "You know how when you're alive you think some things are so important? Well, they aren't, not in the big time. And when you're dead, people say that all your troubles are over? Not hardly."

"Come on, where does he hang out when he's not flitting around like a bat or breaking the speed limit in a fancy car?"

Elise shrugged. "Somewhere up at the north end of town. He never told me exactly."

"Do you remember what you said about setting you free? Do you still want it?"

"Yes," she said very quietly. "A stake through the heart will make me all the way dead."

She paused. "I was hoping you would do it for me."

Wonderful, I thought. *She's not just a vampire, she's a suicidal vampire. Dad's going to love hearing about this.*

"Give me Mr. Grey," I said, "and I'll do it."

She paused. I could hear my own breathing, but she was silent. I hated what I was doing to her. A real friend wouldn't make a friend jump through hoops to get help.

Well, I did it anyway.

She looked at me for a moment. "You really do mean to go after him, don't you?"

"I'm going to try."

"You'll have to do it during daylight," she said. "Anything else is too dangerous. And I don't know where he sleeps."

"Find out for me. Tell me where he keeps his coffin, and I'll do whatever it takes to set you free."

Elise didn't have to think about that for very long. "I can find out his resting place for you tonight."

"How will you let me know the address?" An annoying practical consideration, but I couldn't help Elise without it.

"I'll find a way," she said. "Then you find a way to help me." She paused. "And whatever you do, *don't let him in*."

And she vanished. Not a sudden disappearance, but a drifting away into motes of dust that sparkled briefly in the beam of the flashlight. Then she was gone.

Chapter Nine

I WENT back to the car. I had enough presence of mind left to wipe the front doorknob with the tail of my shirt, and to be glad I hadn't touched anything else. Sooner or later the police would find what I'd found, and I didn't need my fingerprints all over a murder scene. I had enough problems without that.

I drove for almost thirty minutes before stopping at a pay phone in a neighborhood on the other side of town. I dialed 911.

"There's something funny going on at 853 Abercrombie Terrace," I said. "I think they have a prowler."

Then I hung up. I didn't know what kind of priority the police would give to an anonymous phone call like that one, but they were sure to check it out eventually. And after they did, people would come with stretchers and body bags, and take Mr. and Mrs. Barbizon away. It wasn't much of a thing to do for Elise's parents, but it was all I could think of. And it was nothing beside the favor I'd promised to do for Elise.

My house was dark when I got back; Dad and Regina were still out. Inside, the light was flashing on the answering machine. It was Freddie. "Got your message," his voice said on the tape. "Don't do anything without me."

"Too late," I muttered, and erased the call.

I had to work until eleven to finish my homework. It isn't that I'm the studious type, or a teacher's pet or anything, but right then I didn't want to do anything more adventurous than sit under a bright light and keep my mind busy with the sort of problems that had nice tidy answers. I definitely didn't want to think about what I'd seen at the Barbizons' house, or about the mysterious Mr. Grey—or about the deal I'd made with Elise. I couldn't seem to stop thinking about it, though, and eventually the thinking got in the way of everything else.

"I need to talk to someone," I muttered. The question was, who? Dad still wasn't home yet, and it was way too late to call Freddie. The last time I'd glanced at the kitchen clock in passing, it had been almost midnight.

I thought about calling my grandmother in Florida, but couldn't see waking her up out of a sound sleep to tell her that I was a werewolf and vampires were chasing me. Some things need to be broken to people gently. Finally, I shrugged and punched in the phone number of the counselor I'd seen for a while last year, after the mess with Jay was over. It was a middle-of-the-night call for him, too, but hey—that was the sort of thing he got paid for.

The phone rang six times at the other end before anybody picked it up. I heard a muzzy voice saying, "Hello?"

"This is Val Sherwood," I said. "We've got to talk. There are *vampires* out here."

"There are vampires here, too."

The voice had changed. It wasn't my counselor's voice anymore; it was the voice of the man who had come to my doorstep the night I sensed a presence hunting among the crowd at the movie theater. And I understood: the man in the tailored suit was Elise Barbizon's master vampire, the one she called Mr. Grey. He must have taken her that same night. Taken her first, and come back for me as an afterthought.

I felt almost insulted. *What is this, I'm not good enough to be a first-string victim?*

"There are other needs than blood," Mr. Grey said. His voice sounded amused, as if he'd read my thoughts. For all I knew, he had. "Your young friend Frederick Hanger: I want him. You will deliver him to me. Good night."

The line went dead.

I looked at the receiver in my hand for a long time, while the off-hook signal beeped at me. *Am I that predictable?* I wondered. *Or is he somewhere out there, watching me, just so he can get his undead jollies by playing with my mind?*

I went to my bedroom, but I didn't go to bed. I sat up until dawn, staring out my bedroom window and listening to the wind. Mr. Grey was out there, and he wanted Freddie—not for anything good, that was for certain. The master vampire might have some uses in mind for me, but there was nothing that Freddie could be to him except a threat.

A threat. Right. Freddie Hanger and his silver bullets and garlic wreaths and bottles of lime juice? Lime juice, for heaven's sake!

Freddie's okay, I reassured myself. *He's home, and he's been warned already. Mr. Grey made a mistake last summer when he tried to take out Freddie first.*

I was a little bit comforted to realize that even a master vampire could sometimes make mistakes. But Mr. Grey was persistent—the undead could afford the time for persistence—and I had a feeling that he held grudges.

I wondered if Freddie might be right. *Was* Mr. Grey somehow responsible for what had happened with Jay Collins? Had the vampire wanted a werewolf on his team even then?

Sunrise didn't bring any answers, although it helped soothe my nerves to know that Mr. Grey was safely in his grave for a few hours. But I still didn't know how Elise was going to get the word to me on where the master vampire's resting place was located. If I was going to do something about that, it would have to be before dark—because tonight was the full moon.

I didn't say much during breakfast. Dad didn't push me; he's not too talkative himself until after his first cup of coffee. He'd just finished drinking it when the telephone rang.

Dad picked up the receiver on the kitchen extension. "Doctor Sherwood here."

Then he was quiet for a long time while the person on the other end talked. I could tell from the way his expression changed that he wasn't hearing anything good. "When?" he said once, and "How many?" and then, "I'll be there."

As soon as he hung up, he dialed another number—this one must have been his answering service. "Reschedule all my appointments for today."

"What's wrong?" I asked after he'd finished, even though I already had a fair idea what the problem had to be.

"Something serious, I'm afraid," he said. "I've been asked to go to your school today as an emergency crisis counselor. One of your classmates is . . . missing, under some very tragic circumstances."

"Who?" I asked, not because I didn't know the answer, but because I figured it was expected of me.

And Dad said, "The Barbizon girl—Elise. Her parents were found dead early this morning, after somebody tipped off the police with an anonymous telephone call."

I didn't say anything after that. I couldn't think of anything I *could* say—knowing everything that I knew and knowing what I was planning to do about it—that wouldn't come out sounding all wrong.

I rode into school with my father instead of taking the bus. Dad would be spending all day at the high school anyhow, as one of the crisis counselors. We didn't talk much on the way. I could tell that Dad was expecting some kind of emotional reaction from me, since he knew Elise and I had been friends. He kept giving me concerned looks, as if he thought I might break down and have hysterics at any minute. And I'd have been delighted to oblige him, except that I had other things on my mind, like trying to figure out a good way to tell him what was going on.

"Hey, Dad . . . remember how you never believed in werewolves until you actually met one? Well, how do you feel about vampires?"

I winced just thinking about it. Try again.

"Tell me what you think, Dad. Would driving a stake through a sleeping vampire count as self-defense?"

No, that one wouldn't work either.

"About Elise Barbizon . . . I've promised to put a stake in her heart as soon as I've killed the master vampire who made her into one of the living dead. . . ."

Definitely, no.

But I was going to have to tell my father the truth eventually, just like last autumn when I'd had to tell him the truth about werewolves—and about me. And as father-daughter talks go, this latest one promised to be a real winner.

For a few minutes I thought about bringing in Freddie for moral support, but then I changed my mind. Freddie Hanger as the high school version of Professor Van Helsing from the Dracula movies wasn't going to convince my father of anything except the need to have a long, concerned talk with Freddie's mom and dad. In the end I chickened out, more or less: I decided to hold off on the heart-to-heart conversation until sometime when I could catch my father without other people around. By that time, if I was lucky, all the vampires in town would be all the way dead.

At school, things were mixed up all day. We had group counseling sessions, but we also had police officers—detectives in plainclothes—talking to people one at a time in the school office. None of the teachers seemed to know for sure who was supposed to be in the classroom for a particular period, and who was supposed to be excused. The counselors kept trying to get us to talk about how we felt; the cops, on the other hand, wanted to find out what we might have seen and heard.

I kept my eyes open for Freddie, but he didn't show up until lunch, the only period we shared. I dragged him away from his friends and over

99

to a table in a quiet, or at least not-so-noisy, corner of the cafeteria—Elise would have been proud of me.

"Sit down," I said. "Do you know about what happened at the Barbizons' house?"

"The whole school knows by now. The cops weren't exactly subtle about it."

I grimaced. " 'Just the facts, ma'am.' All those questions about who saw Elise last, and what kind of relationship she had with her parents . . . I wonder what those guys think is going on? Some kind of kidnapping that got out of hand?"

"They probably believe that Elise did it herself and then ran away," Freddie said. "They could even be right. But it fits in with what we were talking about the other day."

"It sure does."

His eyes widened a little. "What do you mean?"

"I talked with Elise last night. At her house."

"That was dangerous. She could have—"

"Well, she didn't." I tried to think of a way to explain how it had been. "She wants to *die*, Freddie."

"She's already dead."

"No," I said. "She's just—not alive. And she wants to be dead. I promised to help her."

He stared at me. "You did what?"

"If you'd seen her last night, you'd understand." I looked straight at him. "Listen, Freddie—you want to do something about the vampires?"

He gave a quick nod. "That's right."

"Then here's the deal," I said. "I can find out where the master vampire sleeps in the day-time—but we have to pay for the information."

"Pay who?"

"Who do you think?" I said. "Elise. And you know how."

He didn't say anything for a minute. "Can we trust her?" he said finally. "This is a master vampire we're talking about here. He could probably make Elise jump through hoops if he wanted to."

"It's not like she's fond of him," I said. "Are you in this with me, or aren't you?"

"I'm in," he said, real quietly. "But it may not be that easy. You didn't actually tell the police about the last time you saw Elise, did you?"

"Do I *look* crazy? I told them she visited my house after school, and that she sounded disturbed enough then to make me worry. And that's the truth, too, as far as it goes. We can meet after school and go do it."

I sounded a lot more sure of myself than I felt. For one thing, I still didn't know where Mr. Grey was going to be.

And I *didn't* know, until I opened my French assignment book in class. There on a formerly blank page, right after yesterday's lesson, was a note: "Thirty-eight West Locust, third floor, rear." Under it were the initials "EB," and a time, "5:28 A.M., November 18th."

I sat there looking at the note for a while. So Elise had been in and out of my house while I was asleep. Once she'd been invited in, she could come and go anytime she pleased. And so could Mr. Grey.

Not for very long, I thought with satisfaction, as I folded up the note and put it in my purse. *Now that we have this.*

Chapter
Ten

DAD WAS still doing counseling in the school gymnasium when classes ended for the day. I told him I was getting a ride home with Freddie Hanger and headed on down to the parking lot.

Freddie had parked in the rear lot, near the entrance to the band hall and the Metals shop. The rusty old pickup was easy to spot, and there was Freddie, too, in his blue jeans and his plaid flannel shirt, leaning against the side of the cab. He looked tense but excited, almost eager.

"Are you ready?" he asked.

I wasn't sure about that, to tell the truth. "Are you?"

He nodded. "As ready as I'll ever be."

Metal had flashed briefly when he moved his head. I looked more closely and saw a cross shining on a fine metal chain around his neck. I pointed at it.

"Silver?"

"You got it."

I made a face. "Fat lot of good it's going to do me, then."

"Don't worry. I've got lots of other stuff." He reached into the rear of the pickup and pulled out a bright red bulging backpack. "I've had this thing ready ever since I figured out what was really going on."

"What on earth is it?" I asked.

"Hunting gear. I didn't really believe I'd get a chance to use it, though. Not until now."

"It stinks of garlic," I said. "Put it back, Freddie, for heaven's sake. I'm glad you've got the stuff—but do you really want me to get sick all over the parking lot?"

He looked at me a moment—it made me wonder if the garlic was only in case of vampires, which made me wonder if I was getting a bit more paranoid than really necessary—then returned the backpack to the rear of the pickup. We both got up into the cab, and he started the engine.

"You already have the address?" he said as we pulled out of the parking lot.

I nodded. "Thirty-eight West Locust, third floor, rear. Elise came through like she said she would. Let's go on and get it over with."

"Not just yet," Freddie said. "We need to get a few things straightened out first."

"We can straighten them out on the road. There isn't so much time left before sunset that we can afford to waste it."

"We have enough time for this."

I sighed. Like I said before, Freddie is as pigheaded as they come. "All right. Where do you want to go?"

"How about the food court at the mall?"

"It sounds as good as anything else," I said.

We drove out to the mall, and went to the hamburger stand nearest the food court entrance. Not that either one of us was hungry. Well, I was, like always—but I didn't have much of an appetite, if you know what I mean. The thought of what we were planning to do kept getting in the way.

Do vampires wake up when you hit them with the stake? I wondered. *Do they scream?*

Do they fight back?

Neither one of us said anything until we were settled down at a table with our Cokes and fries. I could tell, though, that Freddie had something on his mind. He kept looking over at me, then down at the table, then over at me again. When he still didn't speak up, I got impatient. We didn't have all that much time before sunset—or before moonrise.

"All right, Freddie," I said. "Spit it out. What have you got that you're not telling me about?"

He looked away and poked at the ice in his Coke with his straw. "I don't think I *ought* to tell you everything," he said. "And anyhow, that's not what I—"

"We're in this together," I said, "so you'd better let me in on your plans. The last time you didn't tell me what you had in mind, you nearly got us both killed."

He looked embarrassed—good thing, too, considering that I'd been the one he'd hit by mistake with a silver bullet—but he still shook his head. "I'm easier to kill than you are, Val; I need all the edge I can get. And the less you know, the less the master vampire can make you tell him, if things go wrong."

I didn't like admitting it, but he was right. "Okay. But for heaven's sake, Freddie, be careful."

"Yeah," he said. "You be careful, too. If you'd told me what was going on with you and Jay last fall—"

"You'd still have missed him and hit me," I said. "Face it, Freddie Hanger, you're a lousy shot."

"I've been practicing."

I shook my head. "Why am I not surprised?"

"I promise this time I won't hurt you."

"Thanks," I said. "I think." I stared at my french fries for a moment. "Talking about things going wrong . . . I've been thinking. Remember how you said that dead werewolves come back as vampires?"

"Some of the books say that," Freddie corrected me. "Not all of them. What I do know is that there's more to becoming a vampire than just being a vampire's victim."

"If you say so."

"Has to be," he said. I recognized the expression on his face now: the eager look which even in grade school had always meant that Freddie

Hanger had discovered a neat idea and was going to make sure that everyone else knew about it, too. "I worked out the math. If every single person who ever got killed by a vampire turned into a vampire, and those vampires made more vampires, and vampires are immortal, the entire population of the world would have been vampires by now."

"That's what you said about werewolves."

"So I was wrong, sort of. Turns out most werewolves don't bite people at all—they go out of their way to *avoid* biting people, as far as I can tell. Assuming that you're a typical specimen, of course."

"Thanks," I said again.

"You're welcome. Vampires, now, go after people on purpose, and kill their victims. So it stands to reason . . ."

"I believe you," I said hastily, before he could pull out a pencil stub and start working through the math all over again on the paper napkins. "And just in case things go really, really wrong— you know what I mean—I want you to take care of me so I won't come back."

"Right," he said. He laughed, but not as though he thought anything was particularly funny. "You know, that was what I wanted to talk to you about in the first place. I've got stakes and a mallet in my backpack; if things don't work out, I'm going to need you to do the same thing for me."

There wasn't much else to say—an agreement

like that one is a real conversation killer, believe me. We threw our empty Coke cups and our french fry wrappers into the trash bin and left the mall. The late afternoon sun cast a golden light over the streets and buildings as we drove back toward West Locust, in the old section of town.

Number 38 on Locust Street turned out to be an old three-story rooming house. There weren't many cars parked in the neighborhood, but Freddie's rusty pickup looked right at home with the ones that were. Mr. Grey didn't care much about his daytime surroundings if he'd stashed his coffin around here. I wondered where he kept his BMW.

Freddie looked over at me. "This is the place?"

"That's what the note said," I told him.

"Okay," Freddie said. "If we're going to do it, let's go. No point in wasting time."

Now that we'd found the address, I was getting nervous again, this time for fairly mundane reasons. "I just hope we don't get arrested."

"Act like you belong here," Freddie said. "No one will look at you twice."

He parked the truck on the street around the corner and pulled his backpack out of the rear. I watched uneasily as he shrugged it on. It still smelled of garlic.

"Keep that thing away from me, okay?"

"As much as I can. But I may need all of the stuff in here before we're finished."

I stared at him. " 'May?' "

"I've never actually done this before, remember? And you can't always depend on the textbooks."

Well, *that* was true, anyhow. "All right," I said. "Let's go."

We climbed the steps to the front porch of the rooming house, turned the knob, and went in. The right side of the foyer held mailboxes, the narrow indoor kind with battered-looking combination locks. On the left side a stairway led to the upper floors. Most of the light in the foyer came from through the glass pane in the front door.

I had an unpleasant thought. "Suppose our friend has already—already turned everyone else in the house. What if we're trapped and surrounded?"

Freddie shook his head. "It wouldn't make sense for him to do something like that."

I didn't find his argument comforting. What made sense to Freddie and what made sense to everybody else in the world didn't always match up very exactly—and what would make sense to a master vampire was anybody's guess.

"Besides," he added, "it's daylight. We're safe until the sun goes down, no matter what happens."

In any case, we made it to the third floor without seeing or hearing another person, living or undead. Freddie put down his backpack and pulled out a mallet and a wooden stake. He thrust them in my direction.

"Here. Hold these while I get us in."

I took the stake and the mallet. They felt heavy and clumsy in my awkward grip. "I didn't know you'd studied breaking and entering," I said to Freddie.

"When I was in fifth grade I wanted to be a spy," he said. He was playing around with the door lock and a thin strip of plastic out of his backpack. "I taught myself a whole bunch of useful stuff."

There was a "click" from the lock. Freddie put his shoulder against the door and pushed it open.

"If you keep pressure on the hinges, they don't squeak," he whispered. "I've done my reading."

He dug into the pack again and came up with a flashlight. Then he picked up the backpack by one strap with his other hand and said, "Let's go on in."

The flashlight came in handy: with the door closed behind us, the room was pitch-black. Some-one had unscrewed the light bulb from the socket in the ceiling and taped sheets of aluminum foil over the windows. I wondered if Mr. Grey had done that bit of vampiric housekeeping himself—or had Elise done it for him by daylight, before she changed?

It only took us a few minutes to walk through the entire apartment: two rooms with a connecting hall and a closet, all empty. No furniture, just bare rooms that looked like no one had been in them for months. Our sneakers left tread marks on the dusty floorboards.

And there wasn't a coffin, or anything remotely resembling one. Nothing large enough for a body to lie in. But even with my human nose, and even with the garlic in Freddie's backpack stinking up everything, I could smell the characteristic vampire odor—the dead-and-buried stench that I'd caught on the wind last time I ran in wolf-shape, the same one I'd smelled all over the Barbizon house.

"Are you sure this is the right place?" Freddie asked, after we'd been through all the rooms. "I never did think we could trust—"

"This is the place," I said. "I don't know where the vampire is now, but he's been in here, all right."

"Well, he sure isn't here now," said Freddie. He flashed the beam of his light around the corners of the room to emphasize his point. "Nothing but dust and cobwebs."

"Wait a minute," I said. The bar of light had skidded past something white and crumpled in the far corner. "What's that?"

"Piece of paper, looks like." Freddie picked the wrinkled scrap up off the floor and smoothed it out. When he looked at it more closely, his eyes got a kind of enthusiastic glow. "What do you know—a rental agreement. An address on North Clark. Maybe our vamp has moved."

"This is starting to feel like a scavenger hunt," I complained. "Why do I get the feeling we're going to do some more breaking and entering?"

"If we have to," said Freddie. "Come on, let's go. Daylight's wasting."

We drove over to North Clark. It wasn't far—both West Locust and North Clark were in the old part of town, where the Victorian houses from the city's first building boom were still standing. North Clark was a bit better neighborhood than Locust; not as nice as the professional district where my dad had his office, but almost. Naturally, the address we were looking for turned out to be the most run-down house on the whole street—not quite decrepit enough to look haunted, but close.

As far as I could see, the big two-story building didn't have anybody living in it, and hadn't for quite some time. The yard looked like somebody from a gardening service went over it with a lawn mower about once a month, just often enough to keep the place from turning into a public disgrace. Nobody was getting paid to do anything about the trees and shrubbery, though; the house sat in the middle of an overgrown tangle, and the whole thing looked like a starter home for a pair of Addams Family newlyweds.

"There it is," said Freddie. "And the sun isn't down yet."

"We'd better hurry just the same," I said.

The drive from Locust to North Clark hadn't taken that long, but it had taken long enough for me to feel the first distracting tug of the coming moonrise. I had some time yet before the change, if I could keep my head clear, but in between me and the full moon was a sunset, and at least an hour of darkness.

"We've got time," said Freddie.

"I hope. Are you planning to do your junior spy routine again for this one?"

"Not if I can help it," he said. "Too public. Let's look around first."

We circled the building. There was a cellar door on the south side, sheltered from the street by a tangle of overgrown rosebushes along the wrought-iron fence. Freddie tried the door; it was unlocked.

"Almost as if someone wanted us to get inside," Freddie said. He pulled the flashlight out of his pack again, pulled the door all the way open, and started down the inside stairs. I followed, brushing off spiderwebs. A wooden door at the bottom of the stone steps wasn't locked either.

"Basement," said Freddie. "In we go."

He pushed the door open. The vampire smell was back, stronger than before, rolling out at us from the darkened basement, overpowering the usual smells of wood rot and wet concrete with its reek of carrion. I tried breathing through my mouth. Freddie was busy shining his flashlight all over the place; he didn't seem to notice the stink at all.

"Let's see," he muttered. "Furnace, water heater . . . nothing that looks like a coffin . . . stairs leading up . . . deep freeze . . . going to have to look upstairs. It doesn't look like he's down here."

113

"Wait a minute," I said. "What did you say?"

"I said, 'It doesn't look like he's down here.' Why?"

"No, about the deep freeze," I said. "Over there."

The freezer occupied the darkest corner of the basement. It was long enough to hold a body, and its lid was still in place—even though whenever you leave one of those things abandoned somewhere, you're supposed to take the top off, so no one will get trapped inside. The top wasn't dusty, either.

I walked over and put my hand on the latch. "Ready?"

Freddie just nodded and handed me the flashlight. He had his hammer in one hand and the stake in the other, and his face looked a lot paler than it had before.

"Okay," I said. "I'm opening it—now."

I heaved on the lid and pushed it back against the wall. A wave of sickening odor welled out, a mixture of rotten meat and vampire mold. The freezer had been a coffin, all right, and there was a fanged vampire inside. But some other vampire hunter had gotten to it first . . . a stake protruded from the center of the vampire's chest, and the body lay half-submerged in congealing blood.

114

Chapter Eleven

FREDDIE'S VOICE sounded choked and tight. "Let's get out of here."

"Right," I said. I didn't sound any better myself. The flashlight was wavering in my hand, which didn't help, with the shadows moving around in that freezer. Mr. Grey—or whoever was in there—wasn't looking too good. Bloated body, peeling skin, black protruding tongue—the whole thing was gross. And the smell was worse.

I let the lid swing shut. That took away the sight, but not the smell. "There's nothing left to do here. Let's go."

We went back up the cellar steps without saying anything to each other. It had gotten closer to sunset while we were down there—the steps themselves lay in deep shadow, and the afternoon light was coming at a low angle through the trees. A layer of flat grey clouds covered the whole sky.

Freddie shut the cellar door behind us, and we walked, still without talking, to where he'd parked the truck. I got in on the passenger side and leaned my head on the dashboard.

Freddie turned the key in the ignition and got the pickup moving. "Looks like the big guy is already staked out," he said. "And we didn't do it."

"I still have to keep my promise to Elise," I said. "You don't have to help if you don't want to."

"Never mind Elise," Freddie said. "I want to know—who did in the master vampire if it wasn't us? Because he sure didn't do it to himself."

"We can figure that out later," I said uneasily. "Right now we need to get going—I have to be back home before moonrise."

"How long have we got?"

I knew the answer to that without having to think—I've practically memorized the relevant pages of the almanac. "Moonrise is at 6:04 P.M."

"No problem," said Freddie. "I can get you home, then get home myself. With what I've got in my pack I should be able to keep any leftover vamps away from us even after sundown."

I sat up straight all of a sudden. Thinking about Freddie's backpack made me realize something: the garlic smell wasn't hanging around the pickup anymore. For a while my nose had been too full of vampire-stink to notice, but now

116

my head was almost clear. "Freddie, where *is* your backpack?"

There was a long pause. "Uh-oh," Freddie said. "I think I left it in the basement."

I closed my eyes. "Oh, wonderful. When the police find a corpse with a stake through its heart, your backpack is going to be right there at the scene of the crime. We have to go back and get it."

"You mean right now?"

"There's time if we hurry," I said. "And I don't want you to get thrown in jail for this." Especially when the first thing he'd probably do when he got there was start talking about werewolves and vampires—I didn't want my secret life to show up on the front page of every tabloid newspaper in every grocery-store checkout line in America.

"Come on," I said. "Let's get it while there's still time."

When we got back to the house on North Clark, the sun was just about to dip below the hills to the west, and I could feel the moon getting nearer beneath the eastern horizon. We made our way across the overgrown lawn to the shadowed ground beside the house, where the cellar door lay waiting. I grabbed the metal door—it was cold under my fingers—and pulled it open. Then I turned on my light.

The smell was still there. I started breathing through my mouth. The basement looked so normal, but I knew what the deep freeze contained. On the floor beside the deep freeze was a little splash of bright color: Freddie's backpack.

"Let's get it and go," I said. My mouth felt tight; I didn't want to breathe the foul air any more than I had to. The picture of what was in that freezer hung in front of my eyes.

The picture . . . my stomach did a sudden queasy roll. "Freddie," I said. I took a step backward, almost bumping into him. "We've been hoaxed. The body in the freezer had dark hair. Mr. Grey—the master vampire—didn't."

We stared at each other for an instant. Then Freddie grabbed his pack and we started back toward the stairs at a run. The air outside was getting colder, and it looked like the first flakes of an early snowfall were blowing down the open cellar door into the basement.

Then I saw that it wasn't snowflakes, but fine motes of dust that were floating in the beam of our flashlight. The dust was coalescing into a human form. Freddie started digging through his pack. I couldn't move—the dust was becoming a solid shape as I watched. Another moment, and Mr. Grey stood at the bottom of the cellar steps, blocking our path.

He spoke. "Valerie, hold him."

I could move again, but only to step behind Freddie and wrap my arms around him, pulling him backwards. He dropped his pack; his flashlight fell onto the floor.

I'm strong. All werewolves are strong. Freddie tried to break free, but I held him fast.

118

"You've done well, Valerie," Mr. Grey said. "I asked you to bring Mr. Hanger to me—and see, here he is."

That was when I learned about being afraid.

I'd thought, after everything that had already happened in my life, becoming a lycanthrope and all, that the worst had happened.

I was wrong.

Sure, when you're still in junior high and think that nothing can hurt you, finding out that some things can outright kill you is bad. But when you're a year older and wiser—and a werewolf—that's when you start to figure out that some things are even worse than dying.

And I was living in one of them now: not having control of what my mouth said or my body did, not knowing whether my thoughts were my own or just compulsions put into my head by Mr. Grey to make me bring Freddie to him.

Freddie had quit trying to get away—either he'd figured out how strong I really was, or in spite of everything he still had a problem about fighting with a girl. I found myself wishing he *would* fight back; it would have made me feel better if he had.

He didn't, though. He just looked at Mr. Grey and spoke in the flat, calm tone that some people use instead of screaming.

"Vampires don't need to look human," he said. "That dust in the apartment—that was you, wasn't it?"

"Another of my little deceptions unmasked," Mr. Grey said. He shook his head in mock sorrow. "Catching you now is both a pity and a relief—you've been an interesting opponent, Mr. Hanger, but you might have grown up into a dangerous one."

Mr. Grey took a step forward, toward us. Then he stopped.

"You have another surprise for me, I can tell. A silver cross around your neck. Valerie, remove it."

My hand snaked up and scrabbled at Freddie's throat. I'm sure I scratched him. But there it was under my fingers, cold and burning at once—silver. I pulled hard and the chain broke. I dropped the metal onto the floor.

I felt Freddie take a deep breath and begin speaking in Latin. "*Exorcio te, creatura nocturnalis*," Freddie said, speaking loudly and slowly.

"Your pronunciation really is abominable," Mr. Grey said. "And your charm a bit less effective than you thought."

He turned to me. "Thank you, my dear. I'll take him now."

I didn't have time to draw breath before Mr. Grey was standing in front of me. He lifted Freddie from my grasp and half-pushed, half-carried him up the inside stairs and out of the basement. I was left behind alone, staring after them at the way they had gone.

A cold draft blowing across my face reminded me that the outside door to the yard was still open. I grabbed Freddie's backpack and ran—up and out, across to where the pickup was waiting parked against the curb. I threw the backpack into the rear of the truck, then clambered into the cab and tried to start the engine. No luck.

Keys, Teen Wonder. Cars work lots better if you have 'em.

Nobody ever said that wolves were quick on the uptake. It took one of our guys three tries before he figured out you can't blow down a brick house. Freddie had left the keys lying on the seat. I snatched them up and shoved what I hoped was the right one into the ignition. This time the car started.

The sound of the engine reminded me that I didn't have any idea of where to go next. *Freddie's folks, maybe. They'll want to know where to start looking for him if he doesn't come home.* When *he doesn't come home. This is all my fault.*

I promised Freddie I'd take care of him if things went wrong. I don't even know if I can do that.

And then, as if things weren't bad enough, I saw her. Elise. She was standing on the street right outside the pickup, still wearing her jeans and that open blouse, in spite of the cold wind.

"You promised me, Val," she said.

I shook my head. "We tried," I said. "He got us anyhow."

121

"You promised."

"He's got Freddie. I can't do it without Freddie's help. Not tonight. We have to get Freddie out first."

Alive or dead, I thought. *If Freddie's alive, I'll get him out of there. If he's dead—I made him a promise, too.*

Elise looked at me. I couldn't tell what she was thinking, or whether she was thinking at all as the living understood thought. "If time is a concern to you, don't worry. Freddie isn't dead yet. Edmund likes to play with his food."

So she was on a first-name basis with the master vampire. That was a cheery thought. The fact that she seemed well acquainted with his tastes and dining habits wasn't much better. I frowned at the steering wheel, trying to put my thoughts in some kind of order.

"You're saying he might have stashed Freddie someplace and gone out hunting someone else for a quick snack?"

"Yes," she said. "He likes the taste of fear. He'll build it up as long as he can before taking him."

My head was feeling steadier now. "He's a real sweetheart. Do you have any idea where he might have put Freddie?"

Elise nodded. "I can find warm blood."

I had to ask.

"Good. Then we can find him." I opened the door of the pickup and swung down to the pavement. "Let's go."

For the third time that evening I headed for the cellar door, carrying Freddie's backpack with me. As long as I held it at arm's length, the smell wasn't too bad. Elise drifted along behind me. Once we were in the basement, I led the way to the stairs, then up. The top parts of the house were quiet, with a layer of dust.

Just like in that apartment. Wonderful. I dug my heel into a particularly gritty part and ground down on it. *Hope that's your face, jerk.*

Elise moved without sound, and very quickly. She was spooky to watch; spookier still when she spoke so matter-of-factly about death and blood. I hoped she was serious about helping me. The last thing I needed was for her to lead me into another trap.

The first floor of the house was empty, except for some furniture. Most of the pieces were covered with dusty white drop cloths, like cobwebby shrouds. I couldn't see anything alive anywhere. Nothing smelled alive, either . . . not even the usual scents of mice and cockroaches and the other small scurrying creatures that would have found homes in an empty house.

The smells—moonrise is getting close. We have to find Freddie before it happens.

"Up," said Elise.

We went up. More stairs led to the second floor. There was a locked door at the end of the upper hallway.

"In here," she said.

I set my shoulder against the door. I guess the
lock wasn't securely fixed in the jamb, because
when I put my whole strength into pushing it
open, the door came away with a creak of nails
pulling out of wood.

"So much for sneaking around." I shoved the
wreckage aside and looked into the room.

Bingo. There was Freddie, tied up and looking
at me.

"Val?" he said softly. "Is he running you again?
Did he send you in to do something nasty?"

I felt my face go red. "You have a filthy mind,
Freddie Hanger. I'm trying to save your stupid
neck."

"Save your own neck," he said. "Get out."

"No," I said. I was already working on the
knots. Mr. Grey must have been an Eagle Scout
before he took up being undead for a permanent
career, because those knots were hard. I nearly
broke a nail on one of them.

"Do you have a knife on you?" I asked.

He gave a kind of strangled laugh. "If I had a
knife on me, do you think I'd still be here? Hurry
up, Val."

"I'm *hurrying*," I said.

The moon would be rising soon—I could feel
it—and after that life would get interesting. If
I was having a hard time with fingers, I didn't
want to think about what it would be like trying to untie those knots with my teeth. Finally
one of them came loose enough to give me some
slack.

Then it was a matter of wriggling and pulling, and I'm afraid Freddie picked up some pretty good rope burns along the way. But when I mentioned that to Freddie, he said, "If we live long enough that I have to explain 'em to my mom, I'll be so happy that I won't even care."

He made it out, then we headed down from the second floor—Freddie and I together, with Elise drifting silently along behind. When we got to the front door, it was closed and locked and sealed with spikes driven right through the frame.

"Guess not," I said. "Looks like we get out of here the same way we came in."

We went back down the steps into the basement. I pointed across the expanse of concrete at the cellar door. It was still open. "Door's that way. Let's go."

We started across the floor toward it, me and Freddie and the not-quite-there Elise—two sets of echoing footsteps and one silence that seemed even louder in my ears.

And there was Mr. Grey, standing with folded arms at the foot of the outside stairs, just inside the shadowed recess that held our pathway up to the open air.

Chapter
Twelve

I COULD feel him reaching out into my mind, controlling me. I froze. *Not again, oh no, not again.*

"Oh, excellent sport," he said. "Such loyalty. I applaud you." And he actually clapped his hands two or three times. "I haven't enjoyed a hunt like this in years."

Mr. Grey turned to Freddie. The master vampire's eyes were blank like marble, just as they had looked when I saw him on my doorstep and thought I'd dreamed him, but his mouth had come open a little and his fangs were glistening.

"A taste," he said. "Only a taste for now. Putting off pleasure improves it, I think."

He took a step closer to where Freddie was standing.

Freddie wasn't moving—I think Mr. Grey had him rooted to the spot with that hypnotic gift of his. And all I can figure is that keeping hold of Freddie's mind must have taken more effort than even Mr. Grey anticipated, because as he stepped closer to Freddie I felt his hold on me starting to slip.

For a moment, at least, my body was my own again—now, if there was just something I could do with it—the silver cross! It still lay on the floor where I'd dropped it. I bent down and grabbed it.

The silver burned hot against my fingers, but the pain didn't bother me. I held it by the chain, with the pendant dangling down on my palm, even though my hand burned like I was holding a wasps' nest.

And I straight-armed Mr. Grey right in the face with my handful of silver cross. The metal was caught between us—and if the silver had hurt me before, it hurt worse now.

But no matter how bad it hurt me, it must have hurt Mr. Grey more. Because he screamed, and writhed away, and—I'm not making this up—turned into a bat and flittered out through the open cellar door.

I dropped the cross and grabbed my hand. I could feel blisters rising where I'd touched the silver. Freddie didn't waste time asking me if I was all right. He dashed across to the door at the bottom of the bulkhead and slammed it shut and shot the bolt.

"Val!" he yelled back at me. "The door at the top of the stairs! Close it!"

My right hand still burned. I ran up the stairs

128

in the dark, grabbed the door handle left-handed, and pulled it shut.

"No lock up here!" I called.

"Wait a minute 'til I get there," Freddie said.

He came running up the stairs, holding the flashlight and shining it on the door. He took a cross out of his pack and laid it against the door, balancing it there.

"That should hold him," he said.

"And if it doesn't?"

"Then we're no worse off than we were five minutes ago."

"Oh yes we are," I wanted to say, but I couldn't—the sound came out as a growl. Somewhere out there the moon was rising above the horizon, and I was changing into a wolf.

I fell to the bottom of the stairs, yipping the whole way. Stairs are bad enough on four feet, even when you aren't entangled in clothes designed for another species.

"Hold still, would you?"

That was Elise talking. She was on her knees beside me; the moldy vampire odor was strong in my nostrils. I felt her hands unbuttoning, unsnapping, and unzipping things, getting me free of the garments. Her fingers were cold, like being touched by dead things—she *was* a dead thing—but her voice was the same as it had always been.

"Hold still," she said again. "You're going to have to walk out of here wearing this stuff in the morning. You can't get it all ripped up."

At least somebody in here thinks there's going to be a morning after, I thought.

"There had better be," Elise said. "You still owe me a favor."

It was as if she could hear what I was thinking.

"Of course I can," Elise said, as she folded the clothes neatly and put them in a pile by the stairway. "I'm a vampire. You're a werewolf. I wish you'd told me that before. If I'd known things like that were real, I might not have . . ."

Her voice trailed off. I wished I could read what she was thinking, the way she could apparently read me. Of course if she could, so could Mr. Grey.

Just what I needed. I tried thinking directly at Elise. *Can he hear what I'm thinking from outside?*

"I don't know. Probably."

And he can make me do whatever he wants, whenever he puts his mind to it.

"Of course he can," said Elise. "It isn't hard."

Freddie looked at her. I noticed that he had one of his silver crosses clenched inside his fist. Except for that little detail, though, he was cool enough to have been chatting with a friend in the school cafeteria. "Who are you talking to?"

"To Val," she said. If she'd noticed the silver cross he was holding, she didn't let on. "Vampires talk to werewolves, you know."

"I read something about that," he said. "But so much of the stuff in books is useless. . . ." He paused. "*You're* an expert. You'd have to be. Can you go through the things in my backpack and tell me what's useful and what isn't?"

"You don't expect much from me, do you?" she said. "But Val promised me a favor, and she can't do it if Mr. Grey takes you both. Let's see what's in the pack."

Freddie dumped everything out of the backpack, and I got to sit back on my haunches and watch him and Elise sort through a pile of the most amazing stuff I'd ever seen—everything from colored rocks and dried leaves to vials of water and wooden crosses.

"Okay," Elise said at last. "Half of this stuff is pure junk, and the rest is stuff I can't even touch."

"Is there anything in there that can seal this place up until morning?"

"No. Not tight enough to keep *him* out."

I wasn't surprised. I didn't care much for the "huddle around the campfire all night and hope the bad things don't get you" routine, anyway. I'd tried it once before, and I didn't like the way it had turned out. It left me a werewolf, is how it turned out, and while lycanthropy is definitely more fun than being dead, my life after that was a lot more complicated than it strictly needed to be.

Besides, my wolf-brain was telling me something. Running away wasn't good enough anymore. It was time to go hunting.

But was that thought really the wolf-brain at

work—or was it just another double-crossing maneuver that Mr. Grey was somehow putting into my head? Suddenly I regretted my smart remark to Freddie the other day about aluminum foil hats. Here he was, the only one who had really tried to be prepared, and it looked like he was going to be the one to suffer.

But *hunting* again. It seemed right. Maybe there was a reason the wolf-thoughts were welling up, trying to take over. Maybe it was a different kind of instinct, for a different kind of self-defense. Time to try something.

Elise, what did I just think?

"Something about aluminum foil hats," she said.

"I've got some aluminum foil," Freddie said. "Silver foil, actually. It was pretty expensive. Why?"

"I'm not talking to you, Freddie," she said impatiently. "Please shut up."

Elise, I'm going to think something. See if you can understand it. I let my wolf-thoughts take over—thoughts of hunting and freedom and smells in the night. Then, with an effort, I pulled back again into the human mind. *There. Did you follow that?*

"No," she said. "All I could feel was a kind of fuzzy blur. What was it?"

Think of it as the Call of the Wild, I said. *Tell Freddie to repack his stuff, then everybody follow me.*

"Val," said Elise. "What are you up to?"

132

Sorry. I'm not telling.

I saw her nod. "I think I understand. Freddie, Val says to pack up your backpack."

Freddie gave her a dubious look. I could tell he still didn't trust her. I shoved the backpack toward him with my muzzle, and sat back on my haunches again, looking up at him. He took the hint—good thing; I really hate doing the clever-doggie stuff—and started packing. I lay down with my head on my front paws and watched him.

As soon as he was done, I got to my feet, shook myself once all over, and pushed my human consciousness down as far as it could go. Down to where I could hardly find it, down to where there wasn't any Valerie Sherwood left for Mr. Grey to find. The wolf-thoughts welled up, images and sensations, unformed ideas that even in human shape I can't really put into words.

Dark place.

Cave? Not cave. People smells.

Bad smells.

Dead things. Dead-and-moving things.

I growled, low in my throat. The way out lay in *that* direction. I ran for it, scrambling up the stairs and knocking aside the flimsy wooden cross that propped shut the door. I ran through the deserted house, still following the clear thread of scent that meant the outside. I came to a place where the moonlight shone in through an unboarded window. *Outside* was just beyond that window—I could smell it, and feel the tug of the

133

moon. I threw myself at the window and crashed through.

Glass shattered around me, spraying out in hundreds of tiny shards that sparkled in the moonlight as they fell. I landed on the soft ground in the overgrown tangle of the yard.

The scents of life flowed into my lungs, but the dead-and-moving smell was still there, mixed in with the sweet life-scent and polluting it with rot and corruption. The wind picked up, bringing the undead smell even more strongly to my nostrils. A beam of moonlight broke through the clouds.

I leaned back my head and howled at the moon. I was hunting—hunting to protect my pack and my packmates, the two others who were crawling through the broken frame behind me. One was full of blood and breath; the other was a dead thing, but one whose death-smell hadn't yet grown so foul that it could hide the scent she'd had in life.

Friend, once. Member of the pack, still.

Now the dead one spoke: "If he's been hurt, he'll have gone to his earth to recover."

"How do you know?" asked the other.

"How do you *think* I know?" The dead one's voice was cold. She wasn't breathing, except when she needed the air to speak. "We can take him now, before sunrise. Can you find him, Val?"

The scent was strong. I could find him. I howled again.

"Sounds like a yes to me," the living one said.

134

"Go get him, Val. We're right behind you."

I sniffed the air, following the scent of the old, powerful dead thing, the one who had never been a friend.

That way.

I ran toward the overgrown backyard. The shadows lay heavy there, but I was unafraid. I was young and strong and fierce. The trail ended abruptly in the long grass. The scent stopped as if its maker had vanished.

Puzzled, I let my human self come back to the surface enough to speculate.

Flown. He's turned into a bat or something and flittered away on the wind.

Wolves can't swear. Sometimes that's a real disadvantage. I whined in frustration and prowled around the spot where he'd vanished, looking up. Then I started casting back and forth, trying to pick up the scent again.

Freddie came up. "Val," he said. "Val. Where is he?"

I looked upward and whimpered.

"So this isn't his home ground after all," Freddie said.

"We've lost him."

I can track him.

Elise came to stand in front of me—one of those soundless reappearances that made my human self so uneasy.

"No good," she said. "Freddie can't move fast enough to follow us."

The truck.

Before she could say anything, I barked and loped over to the pickup. Elise was waiting for me when I got there, long before Freddie came pounding up after us.

She held out her hand. "Give me the keys."

"No," said Freddie. "This is my truck."

"I can drive faster than you can," she said. "I have better reflexes. And I can see better in the dark." All at once she was on the other side of the vehicle, near the driver's side door. "And I'm fast. Give me the keys."

"Okay, okay," Freddie said. "The keys are on the front seat."

Except they weren't, of course—they were in the pocket of my jeans, the ones that Elise had helped me out of when I changed. She had carried them with her; I watched as she and Freddie fumbled through the bundle of clothes. All I could think of, for some reason, was that Grandmother was right: always wear clean underwear, because you never know what might happen to you after you leave the house.

Chapter Thirteen

THEY FINALLY located the keys. Freddie threw his backpack into the rear of the pickup and slid into the middle of the cab. Elise got behind the wheel, and I took my place on the far right side, with the window rolled down and my head stuck out. Anybody seeing us might have thought we were two teenagers and a dog out joyriding after dark, instead of a werewolf, a vampire hunter, and one of the living dead.

Elise started the pickup. The tires screamed on the pavement as we took off. That's when I found out the real reason dogs like to stick their heads out the window when they're riding in cars: the smells come at you at sixty miles an hour, and it's beautiful and strange and glorious. And when I said sixty miles an hour, I meant it. Elise was blasting along through forty-miles-an-hour zones doing at least twenty over the limit, not to mention blowing through stop signs, and generally doing things that would have gotten her an F in drivers' ed.

"Hey!" Freddie exclaimed. "Slow down! If the cops stop us, you can turn into a bat, but my license will turn into confetti."

"Shut up," Elise said, not taking her eyes off the road. "I know where all the living are. If a cop is nearby, I'll know it. We won't get caught."

That doesn't mean we won't die in a flaming car wreck.

She took a corner without bothering to slow down. "I know what I'm doing."

That's what I was afraid of. Because while Elise was talking to Freddie, I'd pulled my head back inside the car to listen better, and when I did that I got a good look at the rearview mirror—the one that Freddie had turned so that it reflected the inside of the vehicle. And I saw Elise.

They say that vampires don't show up in mirrors. That's not true. What *is* true is that mirrors don't have minds to cloud with illusion; all they can show is reality. The face that I saw in the mirror belonged to a week-old corpse: eyeballs starting to collapse inward; lips peeled away from teeth all the way around; pallid flesh smeared with patches of slimy, whitish mold.

No wonder Elise had broken every mirror in her house. Maybe that's when she decided she'd made a bad deal—when she found out what she really looked like. For myself, I turned my head back out the window, so she wouldn't catch me staring at her.

138

Then it came on the breeze—the scent of the master vampire. Somewhere outside. I barked and pointed with my head in the direction of the smell.

"Mark that one, Freddie," Elise said. If I looked at her and not the mirror, she looked the same as she always had, back when we were sharing lunchroom gossip at Hillside High. "I'm going to hunt for more locations. He's tricky."

"No kidding," Freddie said. "How long do you think it'll take him to recover from that face full of silver cross?"

"Long enough, if we hurry," she said, and drove even faster than before.

And so we cruised through the night, as the moon got higher, then started to sink again. I caught sniffs of the vampire smell several more times. At last Freddie said, "I think we've got the neighborhood narrowed down."

"Good," Elise said. "Now for the last bit. We have to find his grave."

"Take us back to Locust and Comstock," Freddie said. "If you draw lines connecting all the places Val scented him, that's where they cross. If you'll pardon the expression."

Elise put us into another screeching turn. "Everybody's a comedian," she said. "When we've finished, you can take your bag of tricks and go home. The rest is between Val and me."

I'm ready, I thought.

Then I let myself sink down into the wolf-mind again, letting the wordless hunting thoughts

139

rise up and make their barrier between my human self and the cold minds of the moving dead ones.

I leapt from the truck as soon as it came to a halt. I didn't know the neighborhood; I'd never hunted here before. But the vampire smell was all over everything.

Freddie was beside me, the pack on his back, carrying a flashlight in one hand and a cross in the other. I looked around and sniffed. No Elise. I whimpered in confusion . . . then the wind shifted and I understood. She didn't want anybody else to see her. And up ahead of us, in the silence of the night, an even more silent shadow was waiting.

Threat, said the wolf-mind, and I advanced, hackles raised, teeth bared, growling. Freddie was right behind me, holding out that cross of his.

In the glow of Freddie's flashlight, the shadow resolved into a man, not tall, but compactly built, with a small dark mustache and a ruddy complexion. No stranger, either, but somebody I knew:

Jonathan Polidori.

The vampire scent was strong on him. But Regina's brother was covered all over with flecks of blood, and the smell was even stronger from those. I recognized *that* smell—it belonged to the body in the freezer.

I let my human self slide out from under the wolf-mind for a bit. I wanted to hear what was going on—and not just hear it, but understand.

"Put that silly thing away," the man was saying. "It doesn't work."

Elise didn't put it in the junk pile, I thought. *And Mr. Grey sure didn't.*

But Freddie couldn't hear me thinking, and Elise wasn't there to pass things along.

Just like the undead. Never around when you need them.

Freddie lowered his arm. "Who are you?" he asked.

"I could ask the same thing," the man said. "But I can tell from that rather melodramatic gesture that you're on the right team, even if you are a bit on the green side."

"Everybody has to start somewhere," said Freddie.

"Quite true, quite true," said the man. He chuckled. Then he seemed to see me for the first time. "Wolf?"

"Husky cross," said Freddie. He must have thought about that question a lot while we were driving around, because the lie came out smoother than vanilla custard. I wagged my tail and tried hard to look like a friendly pooch. "She tracks things, if you know what I mean."

"Ah," the man said. "Be careful with dogs. They can turn on you."

I love you, too. But I didn't growl. Friendly, that was the ticket. Dependable. Good doggie.

"So who are you and what are *you* doing here?" Freddie asked. I could tell by his voice—by his smell—that he was on edge. Not scared, but definitely on the brink of an adrenaline reaction. Under the circumstances, I couldn't say that I blamed him.

"My name's Jonathan Polidori," the man said, holding out a hand. "And like you, I'm a vampire hunter."

I was so surprised I almost yelped aloud. I wondered if Regina knew what her brother was, and what he was doing. Did she hunt vampires, too? Was *this* the work that Jonathan Polidori had needed to finish that night he came by our house after dinner, the work that he needed his sister's help in order to complete? And what would they both do if Dad bared his soul to Regina about his lycanthropic teenaged daughter?

As if I didn't have enough trouble in my life already.

Freddie was looking at the vampire hunter's blood-spattered clothing. "You must be the one who nailed that vamp in the basement over on North Clark."

Polidori gave a modest half bow. "Yes. But that was the spawn. I have to destroy the master as well. Success is very close; I can feel it. But this is not a thing for novices. You had better stay out of the way."

"I want to see the master vampire taken care of," said Freddie stubbornly. "My dog can help you find the right spot." He whistled. "Come on, Val. Go get him."

I'll get you for this someday, Freddie Hanger.

But I put my nose to the ground and started

to untangle the mix of scents. It was hard work: the scent of the rotting blood was covering up the vampire smell enough to make distinguishing between the scents almost impossible. I hunted about a little, then sat back, whining, and looked at Freddie.

"Don't give up now," Freddie said. "We don't have long."

"No, not long at all," Polidori said. "I have waited a long time to put paid to my old enemy."

"What?"

"I have tracked this one from town to town, from city to city, from country to country. Always he has eluded me. But now, we must not fail."

Country to country? The human self caught at that phrase, insisting that it was important. Vampires needed to rest in their native earth— if they moved, they carried it with them. All the stories agreed on that. So maybe I couldn't track Mr. Grey himself, but I could find his earth. It would be one of the smells that didn't belong.

I drew in my breath, and tasted the night air. This time I wasn't searching for the vampire smell at all, but for the smell of foreign dirt.

The odor of rot overlaid everything. I hoped Polidori was going to wash his hands before he did anything else, especially if he was the chef at the Clever Gourmet. But under the vampire stink, I could smell it, not far away—dirt from another part of the country, maybe even another part of the world.

Another smell was there, too, mingling with

the earthy smell. *Lilac*, I thought, and remembered the moving van that had passed through my neighborhood a month ago with a lilac bush strapped onto the rear.

That's how he brought the earth along, I thought. *He was probably inside the van the whole time.*

I dashed off into the night, following the smell of earth and lilacs. The bush wasn't far away. I circled it, barked at Freddie, and tried to pull it up with my teeth. Freddie and Polidori caught up with me a few seconds later and grabbed hold of the trunk of the lilac. They began rocking it back and forth, pulling it up from the ground. The roots tore loose far too easily—but then, the lilac had only recently been replanted. It wouldn't have had much chance to grow.

Pulling up the lilac revealed a shallow pit. Polidori made a wordless noise of triumph. The moon shone into the pit, illuminating a bloated white shape, swollen like a tick which had filled itself with blood.

He must have fed, I thought. *And then gone back to his earth to sleep it off, like a—like a python digesting a pig.*

"There he is," Polidori said. "Do you want him?"

"You can have him," Freddie said. He sounded relieved that he wasn't the one who had to do the job.

"Then give me your hammer and stakes," Polidori said.

Freddie handed them over, and we both backed away. I didn't want to watch, even though I was going to have to do the same thing for Elise, come morning.

Polidori crouched over the pit with the stake in one hand and the hammer in the other. "I've got you this time," he said to the thing inside. He swung the hammer. Its head made a solid thwack as it hit the end of the wooden stake, hit it again and again. The vampire smell was stronger than ever. I wanted to gag.

Then Polidori stood up, a look of exultation on his face. "I've done it!" he cried out. "The master is dead!"

"Am I indeed?" came a voice from out of the darkness. "You don't know who you're facing, young one. Or, apparently, who and what your allies are."

Mr. Grey stepped forward. There was a blackened spot on his face, small and cross-shaped. My mark. He glanced down into the pit.

"Oh, dear," he said. "You've killed yet another of my protégés. But still . . ."

I felt the stirrings of his command in my mind—I'd been pulled too close to human as I listened to the talk. But I wasn't caught yet. I sank down away from him, into the wolf-mind. Maybe the master vampire could control humans, but I wasn't human. I was almost as unnatural as he was, and my thoughts were too far down under the wolf-mind for him to catch.

Dead-and-moving. The wolf-mind didn't approve of vampires. Dead things had no business leaving the ground and threatening the wolf pack. This dead-and-moving one was too strong for the human members of the pack to kill. *Too strong for me?*

The wolf-mind only knew one way to answer that question. I sprang at the master vampire with my fangs bared and sank my teeth into his arm.

It wasn't the brightest thing I've ever done, by a long shot. For one thing—do you have any idea what a vampire *tastes* like? But I couldn't let the filthy taste of him stop me, not when the pack was in danger. I gagged, but I held on.

Mr. Grey didn't turn into a bat and flitter away—he couldn't flitter anywhere with my teeth in his arm. But when I let up to get a better grip, he pulled the arm out from between my fangs so fast it was only a blur. Then he blurred again—shape-shifting—becoming a wolf like me.

He was still trying to command me. I could hear his voice echoing in my mind, but it didn't register any more than the voices of ordinary humans did when I was deep within the wolf-mind. And all the time he was trying to fight me as a wolf, in wolf-shape; but I had experience in fighting as a wolf. I'd done it before, against Jay. Compared to a true werewolf, Mr. Grey was clumsy and slow and inexperienced. And though he was strong, he was oddly insubstantial . . . not nearly as heavy and solid as a true wolf

ought to have been. I caught him by the throat
and twisted him under.

Then the wolf-mind, which had served me well
so far, turned and betrayed me. *This one has
surrendered*, it said. *Wolf-fights don't go to the
death.* I backed off.

Mr. Grey got to his feet and ran, still in his
lupine form. I chased him, forcing him further
away from the human members of the pack. *And
don't come back.*

Then there was another wolf beside me, running along under the moon. I sniffed. The scent
of the undead was there, but not the same as the
scent of the master vampire. I let myself come
back a bit closer to my human self.

Who's there? Elise?

Elise, came the answer back. She had a wolf's
body—I think she must have copied it off me—
but she still had human thoughts, all the way
human. She didn't have the wolf nature.

*Did you know about the one under the lilac
bush?*

I suspected, she replied.

How many more?

Edmund is the last.

I abandoned thought then, and retreated back
into the wolf-mind. Wherever Grey went to
ground, I wanted to be there, to hold him and
pin him until Freddie and Polidori could get
there with their stakes and mallets and silver
crosses. Tonight would be the end. In wolf-shape
or human shape, this one was mine.

Chapter
Fourteen

I RAN in long, loping strides. I ran fast and hard, and kept Grey in sight—and when he pulled away from me, I tracked him by scent. His trail was strong. He was heading somewhere.

Then his goal itself came into sight. The old house. He scrambled in through the same broken window that had been my exit a few hours before. I followed, and Elise with me.

Even after the long chase, Grey was still in wolf-shape. I didn't know why. Had I changed him into a werewolf by biting him? Was he somehow *stuck* in lupine form? I didn't understand. But understanding him wasn't what I wanted at the moment; I wanted to stop him, as permanently as possible. The scent trail led upstairs. I followed.

I came to him at last in an attic room. There was a long box there—another coffin, I supposed—and an old-fashioned oil lamp on a small table. Another table had cosmetics and combs and brushes on it, and a pair of tall candles in antique candlesticks, but no mirror. Mr. Grey, still in wolf-form, was worrying at one of the hairbrushes with his teeth, trying to maneuver it and not having a lot of luck. I could have told him that he wouldn't.

Elise came through the door after me, a ghostly grey wolf that shifted and melted as it came over the threshold, changing back into a tall, pale girl in blue jeans and a loose white shirt. I didn't waste time wondering why she'd changed and Mr. Grey hadn't. I leapt at the master vampire, bearing him down to the floor underneath me.

He didn't fight back or squirm away; he didn't even try to surrender. I could feel his thoughts—powerful, pressing thoughts—but they were all directed at Elise. For some reason I couldn't understand, he was trying to make her pick up the hairbrush and use it on him. I caught a scrap of his thought—something about hair and young women—but it didn't make any more sense than the rest of it.

Whatever hold the master vampire might have had on Elise when he was in his natural shape, he wasn't strong enough to compel her now. Instead of picking up the brush, she walked over to the table and lit one of the candles.

"You're such a man," she said. "I thought so much of you. I wanted to be like you. But what did you do to me? You used me and threw me away, except when you could use me more."

She kicked over the coffin—a bit of it splintered. She'd kicked hard, and the wood was old.

"Now watch this," she said, and touched the candle flame to the splintered wood. It began to glow, then burn, the varnish on it blistering and bubbling. "You're trapped in that body, aren't you?"

The box flared up, tongues of flame reaching the ceiling. Part of the ceiling caught fire, and flames licked along its surface as paint peeled away. I wanted to let go of Mr. Grey and run, but I didn't. I had to hold him for Freddie and Mr. Polidori. They would be along any minute, to do what I couldn't. But it looked like Elise wasn't planning to wait.

"Vampires die in flames," she said calmly, as if she were talking to a human being, and not to a whining, writhing thing in wolf-shape. She picked up the lamp and unscrewed the top. "You told me so, remember?"

And she poured the oil onto him as he struggled in my grip.

Smoke billowed off of the burning walls, choking me. The heat in the room was intense—I felt like I had to be smoldering myself by now. Elise tore a piece of lath away from the burning wall and touched its red-hot end onto Mr. Grey's oil-soaked fur. He exploded into a ball of fire.

That was too much for me. I could smell my own fur scorching as the flame washed over me. Even werewolf healing has its limits, and I didn't feel like testing them with third-degree burns. I

151

let go and backed off. Right out of the room. But I stayed in the upper hall, not far from where Elise stood silhouetted against the flames as she watched the burning.

Then fire was licking along the ceiling above me, and the roaring sound was growing louder. Far away I could hear sirens. I ran downstairs and leapt out through the broken window.

Elise was waiting for me on the lawn. We stood there a while, werewolf and vampire, and watched part of the roof collapse.

"It's over for him," she said finally. "He's dead forever. Now keep your promise to me."

You'll have to wait until I have hands again.

"The moon is going down. It'll set soon."

Where shall I do it?

"Not here," she said. "At home."

She did the motes-of-dust bit and vanished before I could say anything else. I let out my breath in what would have been a sigh if I'd been in human shape, and started out on the long trek back across town to the Barbizon house.

It was almost moonset when I got there, but it looked like no one was around. No one living, at any rate—to my wolf's nose, the vampire stink was all over the place. A band of yellow plastic tape across the door, and another one across the front of the driveway, proclaimed this to be a CRIME SCENE, DO NOT ENTER and a POLICE LINE, DO NOT CROSS.

So sue me, I thought. *I'm a wolf. Wolves don't know how to read.*

152

With a Police Line up, the house would be locked tight. But I wanted to get in—I *needed* to get in. Well, I knew the answer to that problem. I circled around to the rear of the house and picked out a window.

Looks like I'm going to make a career of breaking through closed windows.

I backed off a bit, ran, and leapt, crashing through into the kitchen, not worrying about cuts and splinters from the broken glass. Once inside, I shook myself to get the broken glass out of my fur, then sniffed the air. The smell of dried and rotting blood was thick in the atmosphere inside the house, along with the moldering, earthy vampire smell.

That's what I'm here to take care of. As soon as I've got my hands back. . . .

I didn't have long to wait. I hadn't been in the kitchen more than a couple of minutes before my hind legs stretched out, my balance shifted, and I toppled over backward. The linoleum floor was cold underneath my bare shoulders, and I felt broken glass crunching as I rolled over onto my feet—two feet, this time—and stood up.

It felt wrong, standing there naked in the Barbizons' house. I ought to be properly dressed when I kept my bargain with Elise.

I shook my head. *This is a house, right? There are clothes in houses. I'll find something.*

The place was clotted with the lingering smells of dead humans and undead vampires. I padded around the house, careful not to touch anything

153

with my fingers. The footprints—well, by the time
the cops got around to taking my footprints, I'd
just have to confess. I giggled without meaning
to—nerves, mostly, and the giddiness that went
with coming back from the change.

I went to Elise's room. Her clothes were still
in there. I found a pair of pants that fit me,
more or less, and a shirt that wasn't too baggy. I
was just finishing buttoning it up when I became
aware of eyes watching me from behind. I turned
around. Elise was standing there waiting.

"Your promise," she said.

"I know," I said. "I haven't forgotten."

"Then do it now. Before the sun comes up."

"Here?"

"No. The basement."

"Go get ready," I said. "I'll be there as soon
as I—"

But she was already gone.

I went walking through the house, looking for
what I needed, but I didn't find it anywhere
upstairs. Then I came to the basement steps. It
was dark down there, like a cave—after tonight,
I wasn't ever going to feel the same way about
basements again—but I didn't bother turning on
the light. The last thing I needed was somebody
phoning 911 to report another prowler in the
Barbizons' house.

I started down the stairs. A bit of streetlight
came in through one of the basement windows—
not much illumination, with the moon gone down
and the sun not yet close to rising, but enough. I

took the steps one at a time, feeling my way, and the stairs creaked under me as I went down.

When I reached the bottom of the stairs, the cement floor felt cool underneath my bare feet. The dead smell wasn't as strong here as upstairs—wherever Elise had been sleeping by day, it wasn't here. Instead, the basement smelled of sawdust and varnish; Mr. Barbizon must have been into home improvement in a big way while he was alive.

Off to the right was what looked like a workbench, with tools hung behind it. I walked over there. It's amazing what you can see in the dark, even as a human, once your eyes are fully adjusted.

"Valerie."

The voice came from behind me, whispering in my ear. I nearly jumped out of my skin. When I turned to look, though, I didn't see anything. Just shadows.

Then a hand reached out and touched my shoulder.

I admit it. I screamed. I never said I had nerves of steel or anything like that. I spun back around, and Elise was standing in front of me.

"This is what you're looking for, Val."

She was holding something. Two things, one in each hand. A hammer and a piece of wood— a foot-long piece of broomstick, sharpened at one end.

Elise offered me the stake. "I made this," she said. She pushed the hammer and the stake toward me again. "Please, do it quickly. You promised."

I felt my nerve failing. "Can't you just wait until dawn and go stand in the sunlight or something?"

"Don't you think I've already tried?" she said. "It hurts. I'm not strong enough to end it that way. You have to help me."

"Elise—"

She just stood there looking at me. Her eyes were glassy and unblinking, like a doll's.

She's a walking corpse. And she knows *it.*

I pointed at the patch of light. "Over there," I said. "I have to see what I'm doing."

She didn't say anything, just went and lay down on the concrete floor in the place where I was pointing. The panes of the basement window divided the faint light from outside into grey monochrome squares. They fell at a slant across her body and washed the color out of everything they touched, making the basement corner look like a set from a black-and-white movie.

Elise closed her eyes and folded her hands over her stomach. Her mouth was shut, but I could see the tips of her fangs pressing down on her lower lip. I remembered her wearing the blouse she had on to school once, back before she'd started wearing nothing but scarves and turtlenecks all the time—but there wasn't any breath moving beneath it.

Remember, I told myself. *She's already dead.*

I put the pointed end of the dowel against her chest.

I hope I've got this in the right spot. I don't want to miss her heart.

I raised the hammer. Faster than I could see, her hands came up, grasping the stick, holding it against her flesh—

—*aiming* it.

I swung the hammer down. Not as hard as I could have, with all a lycanthrope's strength behind the blow.

When I hit the wood, Elise's eyelids snapped up and she looked right at me. Her mouth opened wide. I could see the fangs. She hissed at me, just a sound, not words. Her hands still held the stake in place.

I swung the hammer again, harder.

This time she shrieked. I think I can still hear it. But she didn't let go of the stake until I was done.

Chapter
Fifteen

I WALKED upstairs. My hands were covered with blood. I washed them in the kitchen sink, and washed off the hammer, too.

I was tired and worn-out. But there was still one thing I had to do. Holding the receiver through a fold of my shirt, I picked up the phone. I punched in 9-1-1 and said, "Look in the basement at the Barbizon house." I didn't want to think about Elise lying there for a day or two, or a week, until the next time the cops got out to look around.

Time to go, I thought. *Even if Mr. Grey isn't headed in this direction, a squad car is. Time to get out of here.*

I left again by the back window. Going out was harder than breaking in had been, especially considering that I didn't want to leave fingerprints, but I managed. Then I started walking. There wasn't much time left until dawn, and I had quite a hike ahead of me.

I stepped out as fast as I could. My heel came down on something sharp before I'd gone very far, reminding me that I was barefoot. Well, lycanthropic healing would have to do the job. I hoped that it worked on frostbite, too. The predawn air was cold enough that I could see my breath, and the puddles on the sidewalk had crusts of ice on them.

It was too bad I couldn't have stayed a wolf for a little while longer. On four legs I could pass for a dog if I behaved myself. But someone was sure to stop, or at least report, a filthy teenager in a blood-spattered shirt wandering around barefoot a little while before sunrise. The sky in the east was starting to get light with false dawn, and people were already on their way in to work—janitors, waitresses, doughnut fryers, getting ready for the early-morning rush.

I heard a car coming up behind me and slowing down. The yellow glow of its headlights threw my elongated shadow down onto the sidewalk ahead.

So the cops had found me after all. *Stupid*, I thought. *Stupid, stupid, stupid. Somebody must have seen you leaving through the back window.*

A voice spoke behind me. "Okay, you—freeze."

Like I had a choice, I thought, *with the weather like it is.*

I was still in the orderly suburb where the Barbizons had lived—no real place to hide. Just the same, I wasn't going to let the police catch me if I could help it. If I could outrun them . . .

I broke into an easy trot. Car doors opened and slammed behind me, and someone started chasing me. I dodged behind a building, through the shadows. It was a man behind me. I could hear his heavy footsteps. He was picking up speed—matching my pace and then stretching out his stride to overtake me. I headed for a bunch of trees.

I almost made it. But my running style is longer on endurance than on blazing speed, and the man behind me was a sprinter. He caught up with me a few yards short of the corner, grabbing me by the shoulders and pulling me backward.

Another person I couldn't see pulled something loose and coarse-textured—a hood?—down over my head from behind. I fell, hitting the ground hard, and felt my wrists being yanked up and fastened together, while the first man held me down. Then he picked me up and slung me into the car like a sack of onions.

Both of my attackers jumped in after me. Doors slammed shut—one rear, one driver's-side—and the car took off.

The bag over my head was dark and scratchy-textured, and it stank powerfully of garlic.

Garlic.

Already the smell of it was starting to make me feel sick. What made me feel even sicker was realizing what it meant: these guys weren't cops. They had dealt with lycanthropes before.

And they knew what they were looking for when they caught me.

I felt like I was smothering in garlic.

Somebody knows what I am, I thought. *Somebody has to have told. . . .*

My wrists were stinging, too. I pulled at them a little, and felt hard resistance from some kind of metal. I didn't need to ask what kind.

"What's the matter?" said the driver of the car. His voice was somehow familiar, with an odd, nowhere-local accent. "Never wear handcuffs before? And these are special for you, too. Silver."

The person in the backseat with me spoke then for the first time. Her voice was a lot easier to recognize—I'd spent most of a Sunday afternoon chatting in the kitchen with Regina Polidori.

"It's a pity to waste promising material," she said. "Maybe you could use her—"

"No," the man said, and now I recognized Jonathan Polidori's voice and speech patterns. "This one is working for the enemy. She has to get staked."

The "working for the enemy" bit confused me—but the "she has to get staked" was clear enough to make up for it. The car turned and picked up speed. The smell of garlic inside the sack was suffocating me—much longer breathing it, and I'd be sick to my stomach—and the handcuffs burned around my wrists. If I didn't do something soon, the Fearless Werewolf Hunters would find the nice quiet place they were looking for and then . . .

Werewolves heal fast, but not from a stake through the heart. I was just lucky Dad's girl-friend and her crazy brother hadn't fitted out a sniper rifle with a couple of silver rounds and waited in the bushes for me to walk by.

Now I *was* angry. Scared, too, but that just made the anger burn hotter and more desper-ately. As far as I could tell with the bag over my head and the stink of garlic making me sick and disoriented, I was lying sprawled with my head in Regina Polidori's lap, with my legs stretched out and my heels bumping against the backseat door. I raised my head and slammed it down as hard as I could.

Lycanthropes are strong. "As hard as I could" meant that Regina screamed when I hit her.

I didn't give her a chance to draw breath—or myself a chance to think about how much my next move was going to hurt. I pulled my legs up to my chest, then kicked out straight toward the door with both heels. The catch gave way under the impact. I felt the door pop open on its hinges and swing outward.

I used my momentum to curl into a ball and roll in a forward somersault toward the door, then out into the cold. I did it as smoothly as I could with my head in a sack and my hands tied, which means not smoothly at all. I crashed into the pavement, hard enough that I felt a rib crack. At least I hoped it was a rib, and

163

not something that even lycanthropic healing couldn't take care of.

But I remembered to keep my head down and tuck my chin in, even though it meant burying my face in garlicky burlap, so I didn't have a broken neck to contend with. A lycanthrope could take a head-on collision with a Mercedes and not need more than a few minutes to heal. And I was as good a lycanthrope as anybody.

My cracked rib hurt like hell. I was half-rolling, half-bouncing across the concrete, hoping that if anybody was driving along in the other direction they wouldn't run over me. It'd be even nicer if some stranger stopped and helped, but I didn't think my luck was going to stretch that far.

I came to rest, finally, under what felt like a clump of bushes: it was springy and prickly, and smelled of leaf mold. I still had the bag over my head, and my arms hurt from the silver handcuffs and the punishing fall. But I managed to bring my cuffed hands up and work the bag off my head, just in time for garlic-induced nausea to have me vomiting up bile into the fallen leaves. By the time I was finished, my rib hurt more than it had when I hit the pavement—I would have cried out from pain, but I didn't dare. The werewolf hunters couldn't be far away, and they wouldn't let me go this easily.

I lifted my head and peered out through the screening underbrush. The car had stopped some distance ahead. Its taillights cast a red glow down the road. I could see the Polidoris getting out.

They carried flashlights . . . and guns.

Silver bullets, I'll bet.

But I wasn't ready to give up. I pulled my legs under me and lurched to my feet, heading off deeper into the underbrush. I couldn't tell where I was—outside of town somewhere, but how far and in what direction I wasn't sure. I wished the moon was still up. Then I could have found my way home by the smells of the night. Instead, I was going to have to do it by trial and error, with cuts and bruises and broken bones to slow me down, because I wasn't healing properly, the way a werewolf should.

It's the handcuffs. If I can't get them off, I'll just keep getting worse and worse, and the Polidoris won't even have to shoot me to slow me down. Just follow, and let the silver I'm wearing do the work.

My hands were still cuffed in front of me, and the burning silver was starting to make me feel dizzy and weak in the knees. I'd already touched silver twice in the past eighteen hours or so; I wondered if the reaction got worse with frequent exposure.

I didn't have much time. I could see the Polidoris' flashlights coming up the road behind me. If I didn't get deeper into the trees real soon, the hunters would catch up with me. I tried to move faster, swaying and stumbling as I pushed through the bushes. Dry leaves crunched and rustled under my feet like exploding firecrackers, and the snapping branches sounded as loud as pistol shots.

165

With all this racket, they won't have any trouble figuring out which way I'm going.

My whole side throbbed. I knew that if I fell, the cracked rib would break, and maybe put a sharp end through my lung. And with the silver on me, I wouldn't be able to heal that wound, either. I'd just lie there on the ground coughing up blood until my pursuers caught me, and then it would be bye-bye, Val Sherwood.

I've got to do something about these handcuffs.

I remembered how fast I'd healed before, when there wasn't any silver on me. If I was going to do something, now was the time. Before I could think about how much it was going to hurt, I bent over as if I were touching my toes, until the chain part of the handcuffs hung down in front of my feet. Agony screamed in my cracked rib—and all this so far had been the easy part. I had to move faster, or I'd black out before I finished.

Okay, Teen Wonder—now or never.

I put first one foot and then the other on top of the silver chain, pinning it to the ground with my full weight. My bare feet stung where they touched the metal. I jerked myself back upright as fast and hard as I could.

It hurt so much I didn't have enough breath left to cry out. I felt skin and muscle tear away as the cuffs scraped down off my wrists and along the sides of my hands—then caught partway and hung. The silver burned in the raw flesh of my open wounds like metal that had been heated

166

in a forge. I gasped and choked as I gathered what was left of my strength for one more convulsive pull.

This time the cuffs made it over the blood-slickened flesh and fell away. I gasped again—with relief, as the throbbing pain changed to the hot pins-and-needles sensation of open wounds closing and healing in lycanthropic quick-time. The pain of my cracked rib faded, too; for the first time in what felt like several years, I took a deep breath without hurting. I opened and closed my hands. The blood on my skin was still wet, but the flesh and bone were whole and moving freely.

A flashlight beam lanced through the shadows nearby, reminding me that I had to get going. The Polidoris hadn't been hanging back while I took time out to play escape artist. But with my hands free, I could balance myself and protect my face from leaves and branches. I slipped off further into the woods, moving considerably faster and more quietly than before.

Somewhere behind me, I heard Regina Polidori say, "There's the blindfold."

"It's got blood on it," said Jonathan. He sounded pleased with the discovery. "She's hurt; as long as she's got the cuffs on, she won't get far."

I moved farther away from the voices. The flashlight beams played back and forth in the trees behind me. I smiled to myself—as long as they kept that up, I'd see them coming a long time before they could spot me.

A few seconds later, I heard an angry exclamation from what sounded like Jonathan. I was too far away to make out the words, but I could guess the context. They'd found the empty handcuffs. That didn't discourage them, unfortunately. The flashlight beams kept on coming behind me.

I knew I was probably leaving a trail plain enough for a Cub Scout to follow. Once again I wished that I could have stayed in wolf-form a little longer.

Move faster, Teen Wonder.

Turning, I put all my concentration into getting away. I still didn't know where I was, but if I could get away from my hunters it didn't matter.

I ran faster and faster, threading my way back through the trees and underbrush, heading in what I hoped was the general direction of town. The lights and sounds of pursuit vanished far back behind me, and the woods blended into houses, and then to streets, until I was running through familiar territory again.

Then a voice whispered my name, somewhere behind me: "Valerie."

The hairs rose on the back of my neck. I swallowed my fear and kept on running. Again came the sound, as if from the wind among the branches: "Valerie."

I kept on running. Whatever was following me was close—and I didn't think it was the werewolf hunters. Not anymore.

Then I rounded a corner and saw a big glass-and-brick building up ahead. I was so tired that it took me a few seconds to recognize it. After all my blind panic, I'd come in the end not to home, but to the other place where I spent so much of my time—Hillside High, looming up dark-windowed, locked, and empty in the bleak hours before sunrise.

Mr. Grey was waiting for me on the steps, a lean shape in an elegantly tailored suit—just standing there, watching me out of those blank marble eyes. I wanted to turn back, but I couldn't. I didn't have the wolf-mind to protect me anymore. I was too tired to even resist, too tired to do anything except go on forward to meet him.

"Child of the night," he said. "Come with me."

"You're dead," I said. "I saw you burning."

"You saw a fire," he said. "But not a death. Flame can set free as well as destroy."

"I don't understand."

He smiled at me, showing his fangs. "I didn't intend you to. Come, I will take you home."

Chapter
Sixteen

HE TURNED and walked away, and I followed. His BMW was waiting in the side parking lot.

I got in on the passenger side without saying anything, and fastened my seat belt more from habit than anything else; the action seemed curiously irrelevant, considering who I was riding with. Mr. Grey turned the key in the ignition, and the car roared to life. We cruised without lights down the streets that led away from the school.

When we came out onto the highway, Mr. Grey switched on the lights. The BMW picked up speed.

"We will go to your house, Valerie," Mr. Grey said. "No need to give instructions. I know the way."

Mr. Grey drove fast; in far less time than I would have thought possible, we were back in my home neighborhood. When we came up to my house, Dad's car was in the driveway, but all the windows were dark. Not surprising—Dad isn't an early riser unless he has to be. Nor would he have been concerned about my being out all night. On the full moon that was natural.

"We have arrived, Valerie," Mr. Grey said.

I got out. I walked up to the front door. It was unlocked. I hesitated, remembering what I had found the last time I opened an unlocked door. If Mr. Grey had done anything to hurt Dad. . . .

Mr. Grey was standing behind me, willing me to open the door. I twisted the knob and walked in. The house was dark. I could feel Mr. Grey stepping over the threshold behind me.

"So nice of you to have invited me in that night last month," he said. "I took the opportunity to move a portion of my native soil here, to your house. It will be my safe haven, and you will help make this town mine."

Not if I can help it, I thought, but said nothing. I had my strength back now after the long chase away from the Polidoris, and Grey's hold over me wasn't as strong as it had been—maybe I'd broken it too many times in the past few hours. But now wasn't the time to resist. In human shape I couldn't do enough.

But can you hold out for a month, Teen Wonder? Give this guy a whole month, and he'll have made the whole town into a private hunting preserve.

I didn't know what to do. If I'd been a wolf, I'd have whimpered in frustration. I gritted my teeth instead.

172

I walked down the hallway, passing the living room—odd name, "living room," considering what walked through the house with me.

Then a voice came from behind us. "Val! Grab him!"

Freddie!

I whirled around, reaching for Mr. Grey with both hands. Vampires are fast—but so are lycanthropes, and I knew this was going to be my only chance. I threw my arms around the master vampire and pulled. He was strong, but again I noticed that odd lack of mass about him.

Dust. He's been dead so long he's nothing but dust held together by force of will. No matter what my eyes see, he's only dust.

I had him from behind, my arms up under his, my fingers laced behind his neck and my hands pressing his head forward and down.

A light came on in the living room, and Freddie stepped out, silhouetted against the yellow glow. He was carrying a wooden stake in his hand, but seeing him I almost laughed—he was wearing an aluminum foil hat.

Leave it to Freddie. . . .

He slammed the stake forward at Mr. Grey's chest. It must have hit, because the master vampire jerked away, arching his back and screaming the same unearthly sound that Elise had made. But the stake hadn't gone all the way in. It hadn't penetrated his heart. He twisted in my arms, and I felt my grip on him coming loose. There was only one thing to do, and I did it.

I threw myself forward. We landed on the floor, Mr. Grey on his face, me behind him, with our combined weight on that stake protruding from his chest. It went in—it went through—and I felt the sharpened point pierce my skin and ram into my breastbone with a shock of pain.

I could feel my heart beating, the stake trembling with each pulse, as Grey's body lay beneath me. The stake was going to go through my heart, and my arms were still locked around the arms and neck of Grey's corpse. I couldn't push away. Then a hand took my shoulder and pulled me off. I rolled onto my back, the stake coming free, and lay there as the rush of healing shot through my chest.

Freddie was standing above me, that ridiculous cap still perched on top of his head. "Val," he said, "tell me something. Are you a virgin?"

I drew a choking breath and closed my eyes. My shirt was torn and covered with blood—entirely too much of it mine—my feet were bare and filthy, my clothes didn't fit, and my hair hadn't touched a brush since before I'd turned into a wolf.

"Freddie," I said, "if you're trying to make a pass at me, this isn't the right time, it isn't the right place, and I'm definitely not in the right mood."

"No, no, it's not like that," Freddie said. "But he didn't change into a bat or anything. And some of the books say that if you bind a vampire with a rope of maiden's hair, he can't change into another shape."

I sat up and looked at my arms. "They're not *that* hairy," I protested.

"It's the symbolism," Freddie said. "Anyhow, it looks like maiden's hair is one of the things that really works."

I thought back to Mr. Grey in wolf-shape, trying vainly to make Elise use the hairbrush on his fur. Bits and pieces of my own lupine coat must have gotten tangled up with his . . . a rope of maiden's hair, and no kidding. The fire must have burned it all off in time for him to change shape and get away.

"There are times when having a lousy social life isn't so bad," I said finally. "Help me up, okay?"

Freddie put out his hand and pulled me to my feet. I put my arms around him and held on tight. It felt good having a warm, breathing live person there. Something crinkled against my cheek. The aluminum foil.

"Freddie," I said, "what's with the hat?"

"Something you said the other day," he said. "This is silver foil. If aluminum foil can keep out Martian thought-control rays, I figured maybe silver foil could keep a vampire from reading my thoughts. How else was I going to ambush him?"

How else indeed? "You *believe* in Martian thought-control rays?"

"Not really," he admitted. "But I do have a theory about them. . . ."

I pushed away from him. "You would," I said.

Even though Mr. Grey was dead, the vampire smell was still thick around us. "Can you smell it?" I asked Freddie.

"Smell what?" he said.

"Never mind," I said. "I guess it's a werewolf thing. In the meantime, what are we going to do with—with that?"

I pointed at where Mr. Grey lay facedown on the hall carpet, his body strangely shrunken and the pointed end of the stake protruding from his back.

"Leave him there for the sunlight to take him," Freddie said. "Unless you want to haul him outside."

I tried to imagine Fleabrain O'Donnell's reaction to a staked vampire on the front steps. "No, thanks. I don't want to look at him, though. Let's get out of here."

I led the way into the kitchen and switched on the lights. Freddie sat in the breakfast nook and took off his silly hat. He put it down carefully on the table. I pulled open the refrigerator door and started assembling a sandwich. At least one thing hadn't changed, I reflected. My metabolism was still working triple-time, and all the healing my body had done was making me super hungry.

"How did you get in the house?" I asked Freddie. "And how did you know to come here to start with?"

"I got your house keys," Freddie said. "Out of your clothes, when you changed."

"That took some nerve."

Freddie looked a bit embarrassed. "I had to do it, Val. It was for a good cause, and it's not exactly like I could have *asked* you or anything. Anyway, I knew that Grey would be coming here, because Elise told me that you'd invited him in—and I figured there had to be a reason why he wanted you to do it. And after we'd made his other hiding places too hot to hold him, I figured he'd show up here next."

"Right," I said. I wasn't really concentrating on what he was saying; I was trying to figure out a few things, like why the house still smelled of vampires, and why my dad hadn't come charging out in pajamas and bathrobe when Mr. Grey was dying noisily in the front hall.

Freddie was still talking about his newly discovered calling in life. "Think about it, Val. It stands to reason there can't be very many vampires; they're major-league predators. You never find many of those in an ecosystem. So there has to be an underground economy of vampire hunters—just like there are vampires—to keep down the numbers."

"Not exactly," said a voice I thought I'd left behind in the woods outside of town, and Jonathan Polidori came through the door into

177

the kitchen. He was still wearing the same bloodspattered clothes he'd had on before. Regina was with him.

"How did *you* get here?" I asked, at the same time as Freddie said, "What do you mean, not exactly?"

"Very few mortals hunt vampires," Jonathan said. "They lack the stamina, and the wit, for the long pursuit." He smiled at Freddie then, and for the first time I saw his teeth. "Our young werewolf there understands how it goes, doesn't she? Enlighten him, why don't you, Miss Sherwood?"

"Vampire hunters aren't people," I said. "Vampire hunters are other vampires. Competition for available territory. Survival of the fittest. Nature red in fang and claw. Charles Darwin would have loved it."

Polidori nodded and smiled again. "Just so. In fact I discussed the matter with dear Charles when he first proposed his theory. Though not," he added, "in so many words."

I couldn't feel any pressure from Polidori's thoughts on mine. Maybe he wasn't in Mr. Grey's league as far as persuasion went—or maybe he was too busy already. I wondered if vampiric mind control was the reason why my dad hadn't come out to see what was going on.

Meanwhile, Freddie was looking at both of the Polidoris with what someone who knew Freddie would say was a speculative eye. He tilted back in his chair and pulled something out of his pocket—a crucifix, in silver. He thrust it straight

178

at Jonathan Polidori. "Then how do you feel about *this*?"

Jonathan took a step back and turned his head away. *Just like in the movies*, I thought, remembering how he'd conned Freddie into putting up the cross before, when Freddie was standing a lot farther away. No, Jonathan wasn't nearly as strong as Mr. Grey had been. Just luckier, in the long run.

And he had Regina. She didn't even flinch. Instead, she pulled a pistol out of her coat pocket and pointed it at Freddie.

"I think you'll find my symbol a bit more potent than yours," she said. She moved the muzzle of the gun a fraction in my direction. "Silver bullets. Don't even think about it."

Digging down into her pocket again, she pulled out a pair of handcuffs. She tossed them onto the table in front of me. "If you'd just handcuff your friend to the drainpipe under the sink . . . we still have to take care of *you*, and we don't need any interference."

"What if I don't lock him up?"

"Then I shoot him," she said. "Or we can let my master take him." She paused. "And then your father. He's still asleep, you know. It's better that way, really. He'll never know what came to him in the night, never wake up."

Desperately, I tried stalling for time. It wasn't long until sunrise; if I could buy one minute, and another and another, maybe Brother Jonathan

179

would have to go hide in a dark closet or something for another day. Without him standing there for backup, challenging Regina's silver bullets wouldn't be so bad. Still not good, but I'd have a chance.

"If you want to kill me," I said, "why not give *me* to your master, instead of going after my friends and relatives?"

"Oh, no," said Jonathan. "A werewolf's blood isn't the sort I need. And I already know how hard it is to kill one of your kind. Even if I drained you, you'd stand up again as soon as your body had made enough new blood."

"You cut the heads off werewolves," Regina said cheerfully. "And stuff their mouths with garlic. *Then* they die."

In that order, from the sound of it. I felt sick. Freddie looked worse than I felt. I could almost hear him thinking about some grand, heroic— and futile—gesture on my behalf.

I stood up, trying to keep myself between him and the Polidoris. "I'll come with you," I said. "I'll even lock up Freddie first. But you have to promise me, nothing happens to him or to my dad. Leave them both alone, and I won't fight whatever you're going to do to me."

Which was, of course, a bald-faced, flat-out lie—I fully intended to fight them every single bloodstained inch of the way. I never got a chance to try it, though. Whatever Regina was starting to say, she stopped cold when she heard the sound of applause from the doorway.

"Oh, well done," Mr. Grey said. "Valerie, you will indeed be a fine helper once you've been properly trained."

His voice felt like a hand striking me. *Mr. Grey?* I'd seen him dead, with a stake through his heart—the stake that was still protruding from his chest. *Doesn't* anything *kill him? How many times have I seen him die?*

He stepped forward—fast—almost too fast to see—and plucked the pistol from Regina's nerveless hand.

"How did you manage it this time?" Freddie asked. His voice was a terrified croak, but the curiosity in it was real. Freddie Hanger, I began to realize, was the sort of person who would take lab notes on Armageddon.

Mr. Grey looked down at the stake.

"This?" he said. "It was a good try, I have to give you that. My heart, however, is located more to the left side of my body." He reached down and pulled out the piece of wood with his free hand, the one that didn't hold the pistol. "And appearances can be deceiving, too. I thought you would have learned that much by now."

He suddenly filled out, so that he no longer looked like the shrunken corpse he had seemed to be only moments before.

"And *you*, my friends," he said, addressing the Polidoris. "You've caused me no end of trouble. Here it ends."

He still had the stake in his left hand. Now he lifted it up and slammed it through Jonathan

Polidori's body. Polidori screamed as the wood slid home. Blood sprayed all over the kitchen, splattering me and Regina Polidori both.

The sight of Jonathan collapsing into a mass of blood and decay was too much for Regina. She cried out, "No!" and tried to push Mr. Grey away from Polidori's body.

The master vampire let go of the stake—Polidori didn't so much drop to the floor as ooze onto it—and took hold of Regina instead. He bent back her head and placed his fangs against her neck. A trickle of blood ran down her skin.

That was too much for me. Whatever Regina was—and halfway insane was probably the answer, from the glow she'd gotten at the thought of cutting off my head and stuffing my mouth with garlic—I still wasn't about to watch a living person get vampirized in front of my eyes. I let my head fill with the memory of wolf-thoughts and threw myself at Mr. Grey.

I saw him start to change—*a bat; he's going to be a bat, he needs to cover ground and get into hiding before the sun comes up*—and I made a grab for him. I caught him in one hand just as the change was complete. Now, if Freddie was right about maiden's hair, the master vampire couldn't switch into any other shape. He was a bat until I decided to let him go. And I was stronger with one hand than any bat that was ever born.

Freddie hadn't been sitting idle while I made my move. He'd gone for the pistol as soon as

Mr. Grey dropped it—bats have a real problem carrying guns—and now he was holding Regina at gunpoint. Not that she seemed to need it; all the fight had gone out of her when Polidori died the true death.

Freddie gave me a rather shaky grin. "What are we going to say when your father wakes up?"

"Tell him the truth," I said. The bat in my hand squirmed and tried to pull free. I held it even tighter. "Now, if you'll excuse me a minute, I have something to do."

I went out through the kitchen door and onto the front lawn. Outside, true dawn was beginning. I faced toward the eastern horizon, where the sky was growing light with the coming day.

Let me go, said a voice in my mind. *Let me go. I command you. Let me go. . . .*

"Command *this*, crypt-breath," I said, using every bit of my will, and the memory of my friend Elise holding the stake to her chest, to fight off the compulsion he was throwing at me.

I held the bat up in my hand, raising it overhead just as the first red edge of the sun appeared over the hills. The sunlight hit the bat, and it screamed—not a bat sound, or even a human sound, but the long, drawn-out, agonized shriek of a vampire that is dying the last, real death.

I stood there holding the bat until it was silent, no longer screaming, no longer moving. It dissolved between my fingers into a black mist, and the mist flowed down out of my hand onto the frozen ground.

For a moment I saw a man's body lying there, handsome and elegant, dressed in a grey suit. Then the body crumbled into rot and dirt and a few scattered bones that lingered for an instant longer before they crumbled into powder as well.

I walked back into the house. Freddie was still holding Regina at gunpoint.

"It's over," I said. "Edmund Grey is gone."

Chapter
Seventeen

LIKE I'D advised Freddie, we told my dad the truth, and he even believed it. I suppose that once you've made up your mind to accept were-wolves, then vampires don't require much of a leap of faith, even for a highly rational shrink. Seeing Jonathan Polidori shrivel up into dust as the morning sunlight came in through the kitchen windows probably helped Dad make the jump. It certainly helped with the job of cleaning up the kitchen.

Regina Polidori (which wasn't even her real name, as it turned out; her real name was Gladys Finch, and she'd been a public-school dietician in Bayonne, New Jersey, before Jonathan Polidori flapped into her life) came apart completely as soon as Dad showed up. She confessed to every-thing—and I mean *everything*; I had to tell Dad about what had happened to Elise, because Regina wanted to take the blame for that, too. She wasn't lying, either. As far as I could tell, she really believed that she was guilty.

It was hard on Dad; he'd liked Regina a lot. He spent a lot of time over the next few weeks getting her into treatment, and finding her a good lawyer, and making certain that the police—who were delighted to have *somebody* they could pin the bodies on—didn't ride over her roughshod in the course of finishing their investigation.

But that was all he could do. He's ethical down to his bones, and as far as he's concerned, disturbed people are for helping, not for pursuing with romantic intent. For myself, I couldn't figure out whether I was glad or sorry to see Regina go.

"I could have learned to get along with her," I said to Freddie one day at lunch after it was all over. I still didn't feel up to discussing Regina with my father. "If she hadn't wanted to kill me, anyhow."

"That was probably her master talking," Freddie said. "If she'd been Jonathan Polidori's daylight eyes and ears for as long as you say she had, she probably couldn't tell the difference between his thoughts and her own anymore."

"Maybe," I said. "She did try to persuade him not to stake me out—not real hard, but she tried. And I think she really did like Dad—it wasn't *all* just making certain that she and Polidori had a standing invitation to come inside the house of the local werewolf." I frowned at my cheeseburger. "What I want to know is what my dad saw in her in the first place."

Freddie shrugged. "When people are dating, who knows what they want?"

"Beats me," I said. "I haven't had enough dates to tell."

"Nothing like doing research," Freddie said. "What are you doing on Friday night?"